Editors   **Amanda Raczkowski**

Joseph Reed

Assistant Editors   **Tanner Hadfield**

Katy Mongeau

We have a proprietary ink formula that I developed really early on so that everything would be brighter. And now our licensees have to sign a confidentiality agreement. It's typical of a four-color process, but we use a special mixture to make those colors. It's a *secret*.

—Lisa Frank

And how will our dreams, if we manage to go to sleep, suggest the next practical step? Which would you say it was: wild, or elegant, and why? Now as I come to the end of my rope, I noticed the color is incredibly beautiful. And that embossed box.

—John Cage, *On Robert Rauschenberg*

Chromatic

God prayed for rooftops and got the alphabet. Houses were to
come first. Then umlauts. Then love. Instead, it starts with After
and follows with Before. If ancestry is a tracing back, forestry must
be a going forward. On a test: If (you pin a photograph of Artaud to a
tree), then (matrimony). God watches while you rearrange your de-
sires from Aching to Zero. There are _____ species that haven't
been named. If we do not name them, there will never be a record
of their eyes. If I found I could love a child, I'd call her Olive, I'd eat
her before the world ends. My mother is a house. She came first.
Then gunshots. Then love. God is when you cry at your body. God
is what the president calls *a lo mejor*. If my name starts with M, I am
sisters with Morose, Moonrise, Machine. I remember when giving
birth to animals meant a future of luck and hauntings. *Haunting*: an
object that acts out in terror. *Memory*: an emotion made of string.
God calls you terrible names. You still show him your noose. Loss
is what comes after xylophone. Xylophone is how we strike our
longings into sounds, how our violence sings.

The Lincoln Chair

President Lincoln sits on a chair in the middle of a field on the day that he is murdered. He sits quietly and rubs his forehead with his hand. After several hours, President Lincoln stands up and walks into the forest. John Wilkes Booth arrives to find the chair empty, and so continues walking through the clearing. Mary Todd Lincoln sits on the chair in the middle of the field, engrossed in the movement of waves across the tall grasses. John Wilkes Booth arrives and fires his revolver into Mary Todd Lincoln's head and continues walking through the clearing. William Tecumseh Sherman sits on the toppled chair in the middle of the field, engrossed in the movement of fire across the tall Georgians. John Wilkes Booth arrives and ignites a blaze into William Tecumseh Sherman's head and continues striding through the clearing. Annie Oakley sits on the stool in the middle of the field, engrossed in the playing cards she shuffles. John Wilkes Booth arrives and puts a sure shot into Annie Oakley's head and continues to walk through the clearing as the cards flutter down. Charlie Chaplin sits on the cane in the middle of the chair, enraged at the movement of tramps across the field. John Wilkes Booth arrives and, with perfect comedic timing, fires his revolver through Charlie Chaplin's hat and into his head and continues walking through the clearing. Mae West sits on the sofa in the middle of the field, engrossed in the movement of red lipstick across her face. John Wilkes Booth arrives and applies his revolver into Mae West's head and never ceases to walk through the clearing. Gerald Ford sits on the throne in the middle of the field, engrossed in the economic crises moving across the tall masses. John Wilkes Booth arrives and pardons his revolver's blast into Gerald Ford's head and continues limping through the clearing. A shopkeeper from Cleveland, a rabbi, a lawyer from Australia, Crispin Glover, Carrie Fisher—they all fill the same space on the chair in the middle of the place, engrossed by the things that happen after the other things happen. John Wilkes Booth arrives and arrives again, he fires and fires again into the heads of the shopkeeper from Cleveland and the rabbi and the lawyer from Australia and Crispin Glover and Carrie Fisher and continues walking and walking through the clearing. Then come men and women and children from Spain and from Nepal. They come from the bush, from the desert, from the city. One by one, everyone sits on the thing in the location of the place, engaging one thing while another thing happens, as a human performs an irrevocable action into the symbolic operations center of the person. Finally, John Wilkes Booth sits on the chair in the middle of the field, takes a moment to watch the movement of waves across the tall grasses, and then fires his revolver into

John Wilkes Booth's head. President Lincoln returns to the chair, the last man, and watches the waves move across the grasses in the field. His head aches. He lights a pipe; the smoke rises up and up and up. The world is wide and strange and empty.

Trevor Calvert

Leap

At the bottom of a hill a white tabby still jumps, is always jumping. No, not always, just is. Now and is then, is later. Wind crawls down the hill, nestles the cat, caresses the rattlesnake who loves the cat, connects both into a creature that rises above the cedars and pushes into the houses which frustrate the sweet descent of this hill, which can no longer be there, a collapsing, sweeping presence, feeling its way toward you. A leaf presses upward, acts as a chant for creatures with no voice, because I said nothing then and say so little now. The cat can do naught but leap, the snake coil, and the leaf describe, un-knowing, the exact trajectory of then into today, into Oakland, into my hands' chance.

Design

Mandrake, blood, milk, diagrams, geometric figures, circles, pentacles, stone and wood, symbols and symbols and symbols, some cups and some rods, alphabets, ash, purified water, interdigitated scraps of parchment, a cat, a rat, and a snake, circles, wands, salt, numbers, thumbs, a cauldron or saucer, a ghost, petrified wood, books, programs, fern seed, rabbits feet, eggs of snakes, and so much design to arrive where we find ourselves now: near an ocean, in a city overlooking a church, under a sky which in summer makes the roofline look like great mountains in the distance, cold and vast as a glacier as the wind, within a skein of streets and commerce and information slick with its own newness, and finally by ourselves.

Clamor

Try to distinguish one force from another, or envision a civilization that is connected to a sound. Were a single red bird to enter, would its information be added or transmuted? The word "bright" opens a door for the bird, a lens to iris into a room of flowers, into a swelter of bodies thrumming against a dynamic they cannot name but nonetheless resist. Hope, or whatever stands in its place, emanates in the corner as fire, matches the bird for color, competes for sound and adoration, and were we to see it, we still would not hear its voice or the bird's—we would write of it, paint it, and continue heroically to make something.

Gesture

A small piece of nothing crawls into the corner. It is at the end of its line; this is where it lives, where we live, the only place where existence will shrug its shoulders and bear whatever weight we may bring. Perspective unfolds into terrible awe too fast. We've had friends who for this have fallen, who invited these vertiginous angles and edges in, coyly glancing as they walk toward the bedroom. I move my hand in your direction; my hand indicates the gulf between everything. When I love, my hand moves. If I could, I too would find a corner and wait. I would place my gaze into this painting of a snake, wisely tangled, smooth in branches. I would offer you fruit and curl up in your lap.

Chime

It's undirected. Light fades, revealing an environment clinical and unrehearsed. I step out, wondering where everyone has gone, recalling the first time you and I met. When it comes to sound, maybe you are right: there is no forever, there are no operators, only a wood floor which thrums, a family in a painting whom I have never met, a ringing that hovers like a ghost in the lone chair— yet none of these are truly themselves either. If this sound were a diagram, we would know where to explore, and when we looked up at the clouds, we would not see ships or whales or architecture— we would only see water in suspension. As the lights dim, you can almost see it.

Tom   Whalen

Little Doll Africa

I

Little doll's eyelids flutter up. The room is dark. How does she know she's in a room? But as soon as she thinks this, the dark no longer feels like a room. The air in Little doll's porcelain nostrils is thick and hot and humid and reeks of decay, and about her she hears a deep hum, as if insects were murmuring about something, murmuring about her, Little doll, who in no way deserves their attention. Or are these voices some great engine pumping away, away, away, as if in the hold of a ship? Dark so dark Little doll can't see her little finger, so dark she can't imagine her broad fore-head, her nose which anyway is hardly visible, her pucker, her dimpled chin. *Why so dark? What so dark? Who put me here?* Little doll wonders. Don't go into this dark, Little doll. Better be else-where. *But aren't I already here? So how can I leave what I don't understand? Yes yes,* sings Little doll to herself, *I'm already in it, I'm already in it.* In what? Again Little doll pauses to wonder, for she is a great wonderer, and in her way, something of a genius of everything that Little doll is. "I would like to speak to my mother," Little doll requests. Waits in the dark for an answer, but she only hears the pumping, the scraping, the wheezing, *great whale of breath around me, the voices of my ancestors, of all dolls who also one day woke into the dark, like me, just like Little doll, which is what I am and can only be, bereft of mom, dad only a dream, so why ask for them?* Little doll often feels on the verge of a giggle, but it almost never comes, and now doesn't seem the right occasion. *I don't know where I am,* she thinks again, and then thinks nothing, while within she hears her Little doll voice echoing her. And then Little doll's eyes clack open—but weren't they already open?—clack open again, and all around her, as she whirls to see where she is, dark Bush dolls upon dark Bush dolls wheel and swirl and whine like saws toward her.

2

Don't just stand there, Little doll. Run! But she's rooted to the earth, the heat, the dream, she's stunned into disbelief, a condition not worthy of Little doll, it's really not. Nervous, she pulls at her flannel panties, coughs—*cuff! cuff!*—into her sticky Little doll hands. "Oh my, it's awfully hot, wherever it is I am," she says aloud, more not to hear the horror buzzing toward her than herself, and is all the more shocked almost out of her Little doll mind when a voice beside her replies, "Yes, it certainly is." "Wha?" says Little doll and sees dimly, as if her own porcelain skin were emitting a low-wattage glow, a doll shape beside her, one of ridges and stiff contours and a tight little mouth and an extra pair of hands attached at each wrist. "Don't you know where you are?" asks the rigid shape. "No," Little doll pants out, unable to mask the fear beneath her exasperation, "but can you tell me...?" "Africa," the doll beside her interrupts, "Africa, Africa. Don't you know that yet?" *Africa?* thinks Little doll. Yes, that's where she is. *Oh my. Africa? What am I doing here? It's a dream, it's not; it's a dream, it's not.* "It's not a dream," says Practical doll. "Not a dream?" That's right, Little doll. Listen to Practical doll. You might learn something. But Practical doll has her own worries. Here come the buzzing Bush dolls, a thousand of them or more, running on their toes, their hands outstretched, slash marks for mouths, blowing a rotten meat-scented wind before them. "We've been away too long, we're burnt in half," they chant as they rush toward Little doll and Practical doll, the latter standing in Little doll's strange green light, the former trying her best not to reveal to the other how flustered she is, never so flustered before, *but I can't show it, not Little doll, I'll meet this peculiar moment....* Run, Little doll! Run! And with a final glance back at Practical doll squealing and crumbling under the Horror doll swarm, she runs up a hill, praying they won't follow.

3

Poor Little doll, what have you done? No sooner thought than atop the hill Africa lights up, the whole continent ablaze with morning light, the veldt's heat and scent washes over her, the trees rustle with birds and bugs and monkeys, and Little doll is sure now it's a dream, this Africa, otherwise why aren't the Bush dolls still chasing her? I could answer that if I wanted, but Little doll must explore for a moment, if she can find it, her intangible being as she squats down to pee, no more than a thimbleful but astringent in her nostrils. *There it is*, she thinks, as a point in space fades in on her mind's screen, begins to hum, that's it, but the glowpoint as quickly fades out. "*Tant pis,*" Little doll says, hitching up her flannel panties. "Maybe next time." Odd that her pee leaves a green stain in the dust. *If I had my psychology books*, Little doll thinks, *I might consider the stain's aetiology, assuming it has one, but I don't have my books. I'm in Africa, not a library, after all. Of course I might be in a library or a museum, but no, I'm in Africa. The heat, the veldt, the trees and the monkeys, the nightmare behind me, the day ahead to explore all things African, and all things Little doll, too.*

How I can natter on, thinks Little doll skipping down the slope, making dust clouds with her shiny black one-strap shoes. I don't know what comes over Little doll sometimes, she's much too much for herself. *Yes, that I am*, she starts up her ditty, swinging in the heat, the sun so bright it burns away vision, *no matter, no matter, it's all mine to explore, la dee la dee*, then trips over a rock or root—*whoops!*—and stumbles smack into the arms of a giant termite. "Wha?" You can say that again, Little doll, but it won't make your situation any better. "Wha, wha, wha?" Little doll squirms and squiggles, squiggles and squirms, but Giant Termite doll won't let go, wriggles its tongue in her deepest folds and drools all over her.

4

Who would have thought, Little doll thinks (not exactly trying to make the best of a bad situation, more just doing what comes naturally to Little doll), *that insects of the order Isoptera had tongues.* Giant Termite doll may or may not have heard what Little doll thought, I can't say, only that it doesn't hesitate for a moment with its advances upon the matter, so to speak, in its hands. Its feelers slip and slide over Little doll's curves, its eyes leak tears red with hunger, its Giant Soldier Termite jaws clack before Little doll's face.

Oh, Little doll, who's to help you now? "I ur," she says, "I urr..." but that's all she can say before the jaws envelop her. *Oops*, thinks Little doll as her head vanishes into darkness, *oops and gamoosa*, whatever that means, something she must have heard in a movie, which this is not. No, this is the maw of the Giant Termite doll, who wishes upon Little doll—she's sure of it—no good. This is darkness without mind, as silent and implacable as a suicide's tongue. Think, Little doll, in all your Little doll dimness, think. And suddenly she's out again and Giant Soldier Termite doll spits and pushes her away. Precious porcelainity! Of course her carapace protected her from this white-faced pulper of woodflesh, panting and slavering in front of her—you old white monster!—who bows to Little doll, slithers off to its mound, leaving her alone and gleaming, a golden egg in the landscape, while above scream and wheel birds of prey. *Well, you're welcome to that monster who just tried to eat me*, Little doll wishes up to the birds, who pay her no notice—she's not food, not even a morsel, too tainted even for Giant Termite doll, so nothing to us in our vaultedness. Still, she feels a little exposed out here amongst the thousand termite mounds stretching out to the horizon, where the sun is spreading its last rays, reddening the east and the west. Already? *The day passes quickly here*, thinks Little doll and wonders where she might spend the night, because she certainly does not wish to reenter the bush, thank you. Perhaps, then, in that hut over there that looks like a hat?

5

Off Little doll goes, preening and la-dee-da-ing and shaking her golden curls, if she had them, which she doesn't, only this spun-plastic mop of hair that, in a certain light—this one, for example, as the sun performs its last show of the evening—appears almost life-like. *A hut that's a hat*, she sings, *a hat that's a hut. With its arboreal archives and apodictic antelopes, its amulets and animism and anthill of other words beginning in "a," isn't Africa accommodating? A hat that's a hut*, she sings, *a hut that's a hat*, as night settles around her like a warm glove. But the hut really is a hat, she can see that, now that she stands above it, her Little doll eyes wide open. "My, my," she says, rubbing her eyes with the backs of her hands, a bit grimy, she notices, from the heat and the dust. *Must be something wrong with my perspective to have mistaken a hat for a hut. Of course it's a safari hat, anyone can see that. Look at its rounded dome, listen to it clank when I tap it. Maybe*, Little doll thinks, *I could wear it*, though obviously it's far too large for Little doll's head. She bends down and tries to lift it but can barely make it budge. *Whoof*, she puffs, and tries again, raising the rim an inch or two, and out of the crack pops a doll tinier than Little doll. Tinier than me? That's right, Little doll. Lots of things are tinier than you. Ants, for example, or some ants, but not antelopes. Clarissa doll, too, as you see. Don't you recognize her? *Clarissa doll? Well, sort of, I mean, I think so.* "What are you doing in Africa? I mean," says Little doll, "how'd you get away from London and all? Such a big book, so small a doll." To which Clarissa doll, taking only a cursory look at her surroundings, replies that she did not "get away from" anywhere. "I am indeed here in all my extraordinary attraction, though I dare say, if I may, I'm pleased not to see anywhere Mr. Lovelace. I assure you that I have no intention to serve as a delineation of the clash of civilizations. Nor am I here to paint over or perpetuate national or racial or gender inequalities. Beyond this, as if to prove your emotion of surprise, I have no idea why I am here, certainly I'm no mistress of the dark continent, but how glad I am that Mr. Lovelace isn't near."

6

What abuse Clarissa doll must have suffered (death at least) to utter such gibberish, thinks Little doll, still astonished by what popped out from the hat. *Amazing,* she thinks, *when you come to think about it. Whence Clarissa doll? Why Clarissa doll? Where?* But Clarissa doll, her tresses dragging over scrub and dirt, already is entering the bush. "No," Little doll shouts. "Don't go there, Clarissa doll!" Too late. She's already been swallowed up by the dark (Little doll winces at the metaphor's aptness). "Good luck, Clarissa doll," Little doll calls out, waving futilely to the doll born from a hat and a big book. I, for one, don't want to think about what awaits Clarissa doll in the bush; perhaps you shouldn't either, because now Little doll is peeking under the hat again. *Should I or shouldn't I?* Little doll asks herself, as if she had a Jungian night to make up her mind. *Little doll, you're no Jungian, I mean not in the strictest sense, I mean I, too, wouldn't mind enlightening the dead, I mean I like that everything irrupts from the collective unconscious, so I must have as well, but still, I mean…*and then suddenly Practical doll is beside her and says, "Don't do it, Little doll. Don't lift it." "Wha? Practical doll?" "Yes, it's me, I escaped the dark Bush dolls just in time and am here to warn you against looking under that hat there in the dirt, because you never know, you know, Little doll, what you're likely to find in there." "But Practical doll, you sound a little funny to me, like your throat's clogged with cream or something." "The Bush dolls went for my throat, see?" and in the moonlight Little doll thinks she sees a slash in the shape of a quarter moon, or is it a lemniscate? "Come with me, Little doll, back into the bush. It might be the Lord of Death doll under there, and you know what they say about Lord of Death doll." Little doll thinks about this a moment, then says, "You mean about its inordinate fondness for beetles, as Haldane reportedly said to a priest?" "That and other things," Practical doll responds, now tugging at the hem of Little doll's tattered dress. "But, Practical doll," Little doll says, swatting away one of Practical doll's double hands and then glancing up at the wobbly teeth in Practical doll's stiff face, "I thought you *were* dead." "Dead? Me? Practical doll? Yessss," Practical doll sighs and vanishes, and from out of the sigh, Ghost doll reforms itself like some celluloid ectoplasm, then it too shimmers, vaporizes. Only the raw-meat nightscent left on the wind. You were right, Little doll. That wasn't Practical doll. That was Ghost doll. Now let's see what's under that brim.

7

Little doll lifts the hat again. *Why not, it's just an ordinary safari hat lost by some hunter or writer or tourist or movie star*, thinks Little doll, who in no way is enamored of movie stars, no matter their nationality, though she has seen her share of peculiar movies, none of which, not even those featuring Kong dolls, is as strange as waking up in Africa, being chased by buzzing dark Bush dolls, slavered over and near swallowed up by Giant Soldier Termite doll, and almost tricked into reentering the bush (poor Clarissa doll!) by

Practical doll who wasn't really Practical doll but Ghost doll, and *oh my*, Little doll thinks and feels a little faint, though curiously this time the hat's as light as a feather. Steady, Little doll. But when she peeks under the hat, Wind doll (who else could it have been?) pushes against her back, and down goes Little doll into the darkness under the hat, which clamps back onto the ground without a wobble. "*Ooof*," says Little doll, brushing her dress and standing back up, her eyes clacking open and shut, open and shut. *My goodness. I can't see a thing. Am I blind?* No, Little doll, far worse than that. *Wha?* That's right, Little doll is back in the bush again, bereft of light, with only Little doll to comfort Little doll. Listen up. *Wha?* Don't you hear something? *Buzzing Bush dolls?* No, that's not a buzzing or humming. *Is it singing?* "No, it's me, Juju doll, come to your aid." And, yes, there she is, Juju doll jangling with light and smelling of baked bread and mustard and pine cones, with buttons for eyes, a smoking cigarette for a mouth, and a body like a haystack wrapped in colored lights. A real spectacle, this Juju doll. "But what is it you do," asks Little doll, wrinkling her unwrinkable nose, "I mean, other than light things up in the bush?" "Little doll, don't you even see the road you're on? Are you Little doll or Dishabille doll?" "*Little doll*," Little doll snaps back, though her dress is rather dusty, her tresses, if she had them, tattered, I wish someone would come shine Little doll's shoes. "Haven't you learned to shine your own shoes, Little doll?" "I certainly have not, I mean, I don't even have a chamois. Perhaps we could ask that figure up ahead." Juju doll jangles and sparks, rattles and moans, "That's no Figure doll, Little doll," then slaps her mouth and vanishes.

8

If not Figure doll, then what is it? Bush dolls! Lots of Bush dolls! They stand there a hundred meters up the road eyeing Little doll who is concentrating on trying to make herself as inconspicuous as possible. Little doll, do you imagine, as did Bousquet, that you are your own hiding place? You aren't. You're as transparent as Dream doll dreaming. And then Bush dolls put their palms together and from their palms Spider doll plops to the earth. Spider doll born from the palms of Bush dolls willing to mock puzzling existence, what do you want with Little doll? "Just wait and see," Giant Spider doll says, her acidic words sizzling in the dust as she scurries up the road toward Little doll, who suddenly feels her porcelainity as brittle as the carapace of a desiccated beetle. Out of the prints in the dust made by Giant Spider doll, tiny spiders spring up as if they were Gotthelf dolls from Switzerland with sermons in their mouths. And behind them, running again on tiptoes, dark Bush dolls swarm and chant: "Little doll, are you ready for a little vis-à-vis? What made you assume one existence is more valuable than another? Bush dolls want to eat you like meat. Mother of Bush dolls wants to eat Bush dolls. Father of Son of Bush doll dreams he's in a wasteland holding Son doll's hand. We are the dolls of the Bush, we are Bush dolls," sing the mad Bush dolls as they cavort ever closer. And Giant Spider doll keeps coming closer and the spiders continue to sprout in the road and Little doll keeps trying to make herself invisible, though we've told her that's a definite no-go. Not a safe place to be after all, the Interior, is it, Little doll? Thought you'd be safe under the hat? *I didn't. I didn't. Help, Juju doll*, thinks Little doll to herself. "Help," she says, aborting her attempt to become invisible, her heavy eyelids still closed tight. The wind whirls, the air burns, Bush dolls scream toward her. Then Little doll, her head bent down, clacks up her lids to find on the ground a button, a thread, a needle.

9

That's right, Little doll. Surely you must have seen your non-existent mother sew with thread and needle a coat to a button. Gets right to it, does Little doll, as alacritously as her stiff fingers allow (stiff with age, Africa ages one), then stabs the needle into Spider doll's thorax the moment before she pounces. A tautness for a second, then a *pop* and the needle slides in as easily as a knife into soft butter. *Goodness. Did I do that?* She tosses monster and needle over her shoulder, then pulls tight the thread, which ripples along the road and shakes off the other spiders, as well as the astonished, no-longer-buzzing Bush dolls. Shakes them where? *Into the African air.* "*Ahh, ahh,*" says Little doll, "*choo!*" sneezing a cloud of dust from her nostrils. Carrion birds lift off from their platforms in the trees. Crocodiles have doll-like eyes. Little doll decides to follow the thread, that's the best thing, that's what I'd do if I were you, Little doll. Days pass with her on Thread road, through Empty doll-town and More Empty doll-town she walks. Day doll turns to Night doll, Night doll to Dawn doll, Dawn doll to Noon doll, Noon doll to Dusk doll, Dusk doll to Midnight doll, Midnight doll to 3 a.m. doll to Sleep doll and More Sleep doll, until Little doll begins to wonder if there's an end to Thread road. Don't worry, Little doll. Up ahead, yes, she sees it now, stands a cabinet, its wood sunbleached, its door open. *That looks like a nice place to rest,* thinks Little doll. Are you sure? *Why not?* Can't you see, Little doll? That's Lord of Death doll guarding the cabinet, grim as Cerberus. *Lord of Death doll? She's here? So Practical doll who was Ghost doll was right.* Yes, there Lord doll is, all thousand eyes of her, each eye a mouth, each mouth an eye, you can't tell if there's a primal mother eye or mouth because all the eye-mouths look alike, ashen and bloodshot. Somewhere Dream doll wakes up again, but not in Little doll Africa; no matter, then, to Little doll who right now would welcome a dream from Dream doll or Counter doll or Counterfeit doll or Any doll or Anything-but-this-Damned doll, which is what she is, this Lord of Death doll with her thousand awful eyes. All these eyes wobbling and goggling her. It's enough to madden any Little doll, which Little doll isn't—that is, she's not just any doll, but Little doll herself. *"Basta, basta,"* she says, stamping her foot on the earth. "You old Eye doll, old Totem doll, old Lick-Little-doll-to-Death doll you. Why, you're nothing, nothing, nothing but an Inside-Out-Potato doll!"

10

Lord of Death doll shimmers—*old what doll?*—waggles her eyes, hisses, spins, pops into the night. Now nothing separates Little doll from the open cabinet, exposed how long to the sun and wind? Cautiously she steps up to it, rattles the door on its hinges, peers in, but can't see much, dusk having fallen like a sack over the bush. Careful, Little doll. You don't know what's in there. It might be linen, it might be moonlight, it might be an event of blackness. *On the other hand*, Little doll thinks, *I do know, sort of, what's out here.* But still she hesitates. And who can blame Little doll, who's survived dark Bush dolls, Giant Termite doll, Ghost doll, Spider doll, and even Lord of Death doll. *All these bad dolls*, thinks Little doll, *maybe there are more of them. But maybe inside the cabinet I'll be free of Ghost dolls and Spider dolls and Bug and Humbug dolls.* So she lifts her Little doll left foot into the cabinet (how dusty and worn her shoe is, the plastic strap cracked in many places) but hesitates again. Half-in, half-out Little doll? *Yes.* What are you afraid of? *Goodness, I mean, everything. The world at least. Will I die?* Who knows, Little doll? Maybe the seven dolls of narrativity will dance before your mesmerized eyes. *Will my mother be one of them? My father? Am I at the leading edge of the end of things, or just the beginning?* I don't know, I don't know, she mutters to herself, *Little doll of indecision is all I am, and the night's not getting any lighter.* Little doll, haven't you seen how brave you are? I mean, inside might be more dolls of awakening, of change and further change, of turn and encounter and alone. Even Death-and-Transfiguration doll might be there. *Really?* She might be. *And birds and snakes and cheetahs and chimpanzees and all of Africa as shiny as a marble?* Could be, Little doll. *Well then,* thinks Little doll, *perhaps there's no end to adventure,* and lifts her other Little doll foot into the cabinet. *Kind of dark in here,* Little doll notices. Then Wind doll blows shut the door.

Boyd Spahr

Marjorie Daw
(1873)

I sat with the Daws until half past ten, and saw the moon rise on the sea. The ocean, that had stretched motionless and black against the horizon, was changed by magic into a broken field of glittering ice, interspersed with marvellous silvery fjords. In the far distance the Isles of Shoals loomed up like a group of huge bergs drifting down on us. The Polar Regions in a June thaw! It was exceedingly fine. What did we talk about? We talked about the weather—and you! The weather has been disagreeable for several days past,—and so have you. I glided from one topic to the other very naturally. I told my friends of your accident; how it had frustrated all our summer plans, and what our plans were. I played quite a spirited solo on the fibula. Then I described you; or,

Christmas Eve and Christmas Day
(1873)

I turned round; I found a goblet on the wash-stand; I took Lycidas's heavy clothes-brush, and knocked off the neck of the bottle. Did you ever do it, reader, with one of those pressed glass bottles they make now? It smashed like a Prince Rupert's drop in my hand, crumbled into seventy pieces,—a nasty smell of whiskey on the floor,—and I, holding just the hard bottom of the thing with two large spikes running worthless up into the air. But I seized the goblet, poured into it what was left in the bottom, and carried it in to Morton as quietly as I could. He bade me give Lycidas as much as he could swallow; then showed me how to substitute my thumb for his, and compress the great artery. When he was satisfied that he could trust me, he began his rather, I didn't. I spoke of your amiability, of your patience under this severe affliction; of your touching gratitude when Dillon brings you little presents of fruit; of your tenderness to your sister Fanny, whom you would not allow to stay in town to nurse you, and how you heroically sent her back to Newport, preferring to remain alone with Julia

work again, silently; just speaking what must be said to that brave Julia, who seemed to have three hands because he needed them. When all was secure, he glanced at the ghastly white face, with beads of perspiration on the forehead and upper lip, laid his finger on the pulse, and said: "We will have a little more whiskey. No, Julia

Silver and Pewter
(1852)

Perhaps some reader may indignantly exclaim that this course of action was wrong on the part of the Meeks and of Masterton, that it was a compromise of justice to suffer such a villain as Carter proved himself to be, to escape. It was in a certain sense a compromise which, under certain circumstances arising from a certain state of the courts of justice, those, situated as Masterton and the Meeks were, would be very likely to make and would have a good foundation of justification for making. These certain circumstances were that Carter was the son of a wealthy nabob of the city, who would spare no means to defend that son, no matter what might be the evidence of his guilt, and the certain state of the courts of justice was, that a Slipper Vampire would

The Forest
(1852)

The latter was with her father nearly all day—for occasionally he would send her away for exercise, when Margaret took her place, apparently to Mr. De Groot's great content. There was this peculiarity in his disorder, that he suffered from it most at night, the day being comparatively a period of remission. Certainly, one would have supposed that the cares and society of his daughter would have been welcome to him in these hours, if in any; yet it was evident that he rather suffered than enjoyed her presence. Nevertheless, he was nervous if he missed her at the hour when she ought to appear, but as soon as he was satisfied of her being in the mission, he really seemed to prefer that she should be out of his sight. Some of her attitudes and movements around be ready, for money, to take up a case like that of Carter's, and with a bold front, an unlicensed tongue, and in the full armor of legal technicality, stand before judge and jury, insult the witnesses for the prosecution, no matter how respectable they might be, and by hints and open assertion, go even to the length of calling in question the virtue even of Julia

the room, or near his bed, appeared to annoy or startle him more than others. Many sick persons are singularly fastidious on this head, especially those afflicted with nervous diseases; but it is commonly some want of grace, some angularity of posture, some awkward or hurried motion, that offends them. What displeased (if it was displeasure) or at all events disagreeably affected her father in Julia

The Unfortunate Mountain Girl
(1854)

Eltham was thrown constantly into
the society of Mrs. Huntington.
Indeed, he was always among the
invited guests at Paterson's; for
Matilda, though she had seldom met
him during their long separation,
still regarded him as a very particular
friend. He and Morton, who was a
cousin of hers, were invited to join,
as often as it should be convenient,
in their private family circle. Eltham,
who was much fonder of joining a
social circle of friends, than of mix-
ing in promiscuous society, soon
became almost an inmate of the
family. His presence at first inspired
bitter thoughts in the blighted heart
of Julia; but as they had met as
friends during her husband's life,
so they met now. Eltham remem-
bered his early love only as a bright
dream, and he often smiled when he

Totemwell
(1854)

Unable any longer to remain in her
chamber, she threw a shawl over her
shoulders, and descended into the
garden. It was a cold, gray day; the
sky hung low, and now and then a
snow-flake fell through the thick air.
In the far west, a narrow streak of
blue alone gave promise of a brighter
morrow. Well pleased with the
desolation that reigned over all
around, Julia walked slowly along,
with her eyes on the ground, till,
coming to the farthest part of the
garden, she stopped to gaze on the
scene before her. Close at her right
hand an apple-tree stood in bold
relief against the sky. It was the tree
that Philip had planted; and his
parting words, as they stood to-
gether beside it in their happy and
innocent childhood, now all at once
rang loudly in her ears. She surveyed

thought of his waking disappointment. All resentment had long been dead, and he regarded Mrs. Huntington as an early and dear friend. She was changed, entirely changed; and in the melancholy widow, with her white, marble cheeks, and smileless lips, none would have recognized the healthy and happy Julia

the tree with strange interest. It had grown with extraordinary strength and vigor, but its trunk was sadly bent and misshapen; innumerable shoots had started forth from its root and branches, which marred alike its usefulness and beauty; and Julia

Bertha's Engagement
(1875)

"Not knowing all that I am forbidden to tell, there yet may linger in your heart some unbelief in the stern necessity that has torn your life from mine—some vague hope that time or a miracle can change it. Fearing this, and acting from a solemn sense of duty, I have placed a barrier against all such possibilities. We can never meet as we have done again. In order to make this inevitable I have battled against all weakness, and for your sake more than my own turned resolutely from the past. My honor demanded it. The great future which lies before a public man like myself demanded it. Your own peace of mind demanded the sacrifice, and I have made it. Bertha, I am engaged to another—a woman who loves me as you loved me, even perhaps with a deeper

A Question of Honor
(1875)

"What followed you know. I cannot relate, I can scarcely even in my thoughts venture to dwell upon, her great tenderness and gentleness when she sent for me. One thing, however, I must say in self-defense—in order to prove that I was not guilty of the cruelty of which this evening you seemed to think me capable. She asked no questions, she simply said, 'I know the truth!'— and how could I deny it, even if denial would have brought conviction to her, which I doubt? She seemed like one who had already left the passions of earth behind—a calm had come to her which no emotion had power to break. That I have suffered keenly from the thought that such a knowledge should have cast a shadow over her last hours, you will believe—yet I cannot clearly abandonment, because all the strength of her gentle nature concentrates in the one word—love. Bertha, when we meet again, I shall be a married man. I hope then and now, there will be friendship between us. Nothing need prevent that, nothing should prevent it, for the lady I am pledged to marry is Julia

see in what manner to blame myself. I can hear you say, with your eyes shining like stars, that honor should have kept my heart loyal to Julia. Alas! the truth must be written, and you must forgive it as well as you can—in the sense of supreme love, my heart never was given to Julia

The Dead Letter
(1867)

Hugo Blanc, the Artist
(1867)

It was the first day which had really seemed like spring. It was warm and showery; there was a smell of violets and new grass on the air. I had my office-window open, but as the afternoon wore away, and the sun shone out after an April sprinkle, I could not abide the dullness of that court of law. I felt those "blind motions of the spring," which Tennyson attributes to trees and plants. And verily, I was in sympathy with nature. I felt *verdant*—and if the reader thinks that to my discredit, he is at liberty to cherish his opinion. I felt young and happy—years seemed to have dropped away from me, like a mantle of ice, leaving the flowers and freshness to appear. Not knowing whither my fancy would lead me, I walked toward the mansion, and again, as upon that

The road they were following gradually left the river, and began to ascend more and more as they approached the mountains, which lie but a few miles from the shore. At length the driver, who received his instructions from Grey, who was riding with him, turned suddenly to the left and entered a lane bordered on either side by magnificent chestnuts, oaks, and other forest trees, and a few roads in advance of them a beautiful cottage could be partially seen through the trees which surrounded it. The noise of the approaching carriage had aroused the inmates, and a large gate, which opened into the lane, was swung back upon its hinges by one of the servants, and the carriage, following a semicircular carriage-way, drove up in front of an elegant veranda, autumn afternoon upon which I first saw Eleanor after her calamity, I turned my steps to the arbor which crowned the slope at the back of the lawn. Thinking of Eleanor, as I saw her then, I entered the place with a light step, and found Julia

and the happy travelers alighted amid the boxes and packages, opened and unopened, which covered it from one end to the other. A few rooms had been put in order, and as they were gathering upon the veranda, what was their surprise to see Joe Tyson come forward to welcome them, followed by his wife and the sweet little Julia

Control Room

It was when these girls were talking to you that you sort of came to what you called "terms," and it was these preoccupations that prevented growth. They were inhibitors; they removed a sense— "that sense!" we called it—of possibility that should have been present.

I was at the mixing board, so soundless. I had no sense of irony; what I felt was immaterial, which was to say it did not matter. I could have stepped over you for hours and hours; the processional along the canal, the first canal, would have taken over my life at that point.

"The black suit, driver," was as obvious a statement as any I might have made at the time.

The office, we said, was "open," and what this meant depended, as was so often the case, on context. I was calling it "context," being cunning and unscrupulous.

"You're so inscrutable," the captain said, but I had to bluff him. That it would sound bad—tinny, thin—coming out of the stereo was self-evident.

That I was coming out of the speakers myself was, considering the context, self-evident.

Elizabeth Mikesch

Mummies, Next, Mortar

Wet TP is like whisper, gets what song ears never hear even when listened to as careful as any girl could. The only lotion I have got is calamine. The only shampoo kills lice, scalps the skull. We would as kids pick at each other's little lices even after we had run out of mayonnaise. We wet our sheets and set the lice on fire. We wet the dog and put her in the oven.

This cupboard is bare all besides. I am glued to the tube, hungry for hot wings, a wedge for the swelling. I am a nibbler, tug at meat with careful bites, my index fingers sticky. Sweat dricks down.

I am just dirty.

I kissed a flying fuck on the mouth midair just before it went splat six feet deep, under the drink, beside the bones of my dust dog, Lo. Lo who died because her heart was her liver and her liver was a bone she swallowed whole. She swallowed a whole rope and that was what made her feel on fire and that was that.

But I can't be yours, I told him to myself. I can't be your sleeping dog. I can't wait these dog days whole. Could you be pleased to answer my questions?

His tongue is soap and water and as slippery and I keep drinking. I drink how if I do, the bad taste will turn into the shiny and silver poisons that fall out of my mouth, rotting the table and tasting how chewing dark grounds and wet bark would. So I, instead, swallow it all. If I swallow all of who I say, it does not spill out wet. All of who I say does not mess my chin, my neck, and make spill down. It is not soapy or runny.

Would it feel how it feels to swallow a whole rack of ribs whole and swallow way down the blood and the bite? I ask and I ask.

Calm down, Miss. An eel is an eel.

And as slippery as anyone.

I sucked on the eel so my head could rest peaceful. Daylight savings six feet deep, under the drink, beside the bones of my Lo. How soft went that limp city! I found the chests were each empty when I pried. The more that I pried, the more I was slipped splinters. I have bought a lot of tweezers.

I say to him please.

I say, Say it, please, once out loud. Say, do you know what leapt? Do you know what went when you left?

Says he can't see me, but he sure can smell, and I taste how a girl tastes, how a land line stays put, stays still. Says he can't hear what I got to say, but he sure can smell, and I smell how a spoon shines in soapy water.

Waiting will kill a person how ropes do.

I keep to myself lying in the grass outside and waiting for him dungareed and calm how radiators stay in labor. I am outside the reunion. I am waiting for him to stop being fifteen, sixteen. I wait until the wet wedge on his plate stops tasting of a tongue and falls onto the floor so I can kiss it on its lips who knew him inside and out because he licked them like he was hungrier. He licked them like he could stand to gnaw. I wait and spin a radio fuzzy up. I wait how it is left out on the counter with all the lights on and the windows flung wide open, breezing threes.

Why are you an unopened man? I practice singing this out loud waiting outside for him in the grass. Ask him to grow his hair back overnight. Ask him to rip all the warts on him off and stop growing plaque this instant. It is that easy, I say.

He tells me whoa calm down like I could buck him off of me or neigh or whinny.

I am waiting for the grass to itch pink again, for calamine to verde verbatim.

Someday, he will say it but I will know those notes already.

I will laugh in his face to keep from crying how a horse would cry, lips smacking, like he is some ring on fire that horse must gallop up to unscared. Someday, I will rub myself raw, pink, and laugh. I will laugh my belly soapy, laugh until the belly waters silvering, falling out, keeping me from kissing. I chewed at my lips and they are both pretty puffy, but I still swallow them wholly, flying by the two-liter at a time, and still they taste to me of soapy water.

Tapioca

The Finns were mostly our cousins, browns and blondes. They were They Who Play Rough. They would pry cinderblocks from the ice with shovels to chuck at us. They would light our dolls' hair on fire, the smell a smell of a burnt-up diaper.

The smallest of us wore them, sometimes, out.

We would get dropped off by Aippä. She would leave, it seemed, for forever. We passed the hours by the house of the neighborman who took stake in his mailbox. He buried, our cousin said, his brother under there.

The neighborman was from a town called what sounded like Tapioca. Our Finnish cousins down the road burned our hair, pulled us up by the handful, held us swung by the fist. They hid our mittens, stiffed our fingers.

We hated tasting tapioca how we hated elderly canned tuna sandwiches. We spat alfalfa over sinks. We hated afternoon date squares, their smells.

The Finns did not have to bathe. They washed up in their ukki's shack he made. They would put it against us: his own two hands. The shack was a test, a place you throw water on rocks and with your sounds long say sauna. You try to steam out the wuss, try to make it not breathe. You are something if you do not need to lift the ladle, get bucket water up to your nostrils to stop the singeing. Blow on your cousin's skin, he might yelp. You might sting him so he cannot breathe inside the shack.

The top shelf champ would keep you bowing on the low bench if you braved staying. If you stayed you would be breathing into your innie or outie, would be folding.

Bow down to the big boy or girl who would dunk your head in the bucket water and hold it fossilized for you. The wuss would gust out the door. They would run a cold path, swim backward and stare at the shack and pray, backstroke all the way to Bootjack, to Dreamland where they sell tough steaks.

You had to feed the fire as wuss. Open the iron box, black and wicked, scraping your spine, this noise, this croak worse than a frog fried against the grill of Aippä's car. You had to ball up old articles about your uncles and their sports. You crumbled the recruits and the strawberry festival queens and the burden on us because of the lost mine.

Our cousins were brothers and ugly. Their underwear was hanging on clotheslines in the front yard. They skipped school to make up games, to kill crawfish with their boots. Their long johns dangled spew. Täti could not get to scrubbing their gunk.

Our mother scrubbed blood out of her silken slips and under-pant crotches, we had watched. Our mother often got called into the office.

Tapioca seems like spew seems and stays. The town is called another name. To us, it is still Tapioca, what we know of it: snow-plows on Finlander roadnames, the neighborman, carhoods, pylons in the driveway, the occasional parade. The neighborman comes out, sits on the hood, shakes open his newspaper, wears binoculars.

We like to be spied on. We hate neighbors. We hate tapioca and pudding-type things tasting too vanilla.

It is because we play dead the neighborman goddamns us. We lie on his lawn, and one of us crosses our arms over the grave of his good-for-nothing brother. One of us plays pooch. The hamtongue of a dog, a cold cut pink to drip spit. We see Xs for eyes, how our fingers nub crayons, pressing too hard drawing suppertime trout. At our cousins', we must eat dead trout straight from the bay, off wusses' wormed lures.

The neighborman has got no garage, no kids, no wife. He has ice cold beverages.

We hear Would you care for a beverage when Täti brings in the relatives. We get ourselves locked out of houses. We get fed roast under the clothesline. We hold down our cousins' brother and drown him pretend, hold down the one in diapers next. We play resurrection, make mummy bandages. We use this word we heard—appendages. The sissy one plays Mary Magdalene.

It makes the day long. Nobody tucks us in tight. We wait for headlights to blind us through what is called a bay window.

The one Finn we bring back to life. First we kiss his nose and pen his palms, then we tickle his fist open when he won't go along and play dead how we would like. The sissy undresses the dead. The zippers sometimes catch. Dead Finn flinches when his skin is pinched up in his denim. We make fun.

Lie down, Sisyphus.

Reciting:

Bless us O Dog

Give us some snack

If you do not

Then, we pause.

There are not enough seatbelts in our car. The middle ones pinch the chub. The metal is freezing even in summer. We slide the buckle to unbore ourselves on Tapioca roads. The drive takes us a while, and we talk to ourselves in low tones. We play private games when we drive.

Aippä says, Silently, silently.

When we stay with our cousins, we sleep outside under the sky with the bugs beeping. They itch, we rash. Come one bag to the next. The sissy sneaks in, scared of outdoor sounds.

Some nights, we sleep almost naked. It is too much to burrow in our coffining bags. Keeping still makes the glitter bugs blink more on and off for us. We don't know when she'll come for us.

She is in the bathtub, unhappy. She is soaking.

Leave me be.

We'll see, she'll say if we ask.

We go.

She hangs a bed sheet in the backyard that is soaked like somebody got killed, maybe the neighborman's family. Our bed is too small, so we sweat glue together. Spiders nip our wrists. We welt. She leaves bleach out on the counter we think is juice. Pink insulation swigs and pulls our wall. We try to get over the cold.

The Blanket Show

What she does she calls the blanket show. She covers up my shoulders with covers. Those are the given stars alive with bugs. She hits her pinkie to me and shuts off my tongue. I do not tattle. So long as we are awake still, this is how we keep stuck, and we call it the blanket show. Up we go on watching, ever up there folding fingers on crumby, sunken bellies, the toes of us. I hide from her stiff cloth that molds over. To hear her socks skip whoopses over our floor takes a day. I move where she halts. I wait for her to come say out of space—that's what she says to get me. There is us only, no spot for light. She says she sleeps, but I do not believe what she says. She climbs out the window, she says. Stomps on the roof, I am told, but she tells me so. She goes where she goes. The roof I have not seen since June. And so it is, and she leaves me here. I wait to hear thumps and a cuss. She is a rooftop girl, she says. I ask her what I wonder.

That Which Contains Us Is Grave

Age is a move toward something for which we have only thin theories. When she is lying down her chest is flat; when she rises gravity pulls the thick sacs of deposit toward the muted ground. In other words, when she is asleep, she is less woman.

This is her last day as a she. It is spent on her back, in the grass; it is spent in the bath. She is plagued by lashes that work like lace, interwoven, sprawling. They will be her downfall, will give her up.

It will happen in a bathroom in the future. It will happen when she blinks and someone thinks, that kind of beauty is suspicious. Then he'll unzip his fly.

If you are quiet forever, you are empty, a mouth without a tongue, she tells me, lying in the lawn. I look at her through a screen of blades. You are a bathtub in which water pools but fails to hold.

What she does not say, then or ever (what I think when I get the call): the difference between a mouth and a tub depends upon the curve of the lip.

Wolf of Wolf

Wolf wolf wolf wolf wolf and.
So it huffs. Then wolf.
And this puffing also. Wolf:
Of wolf that it should down shimmy up house.
Of wolf then come apart at the shingles.

So wolf when you can get through the woods a meal.
Mealing away the hours like a skin. Wolf.
The let it all be lonely. Wolf and.

Rhetoric might just be another skin to rub up against.
The body a rub up and up.
A determination—we're rubbing ourselves out of our angles.

When you're in the woods, you get out meal handed
to you, wolf. In the woods and move that skinny text to tear.
Get wolving where margin is a way gotten in.

In the woods, do let no building.

No water to wash down the archive.

Neither burn down the woods in search of wolf.

Our children. Where will
our children go to be fed.

= I F (T h e   K n i f e m a k e r

=IF(The Knifemaker does not exist, the story is null, IF(The Knifemaker spangles the sky with daggers, the story is a constellation of fear, IF(The Knifemaker stamps blades in a factory, the story is repetition, IF(The Knifemaker gambles away his riches, the story is the itch of a phantom ring finger, IF(The Knifemaker throws his finest knives, the story is a beautiful woman shiny with scars, IF(The Knifemaker survives the flood, the story is still water reflecting wreckage, IF(The Knifemaker divines the future, the story is the planned ritual of his final day, IF(The Knifemaker lives for his craft, the story is a pocketful of metal shavings, IF(The Knifemaker dreams in color, the story is orange metal & sweat droplets puffing to smoke, IF(The Knifemaker records his thoughts, the story is a life scrawled in scrimshaw handles, IF(The Knifemaker slumps with heartache, the story is the blossom of letters touched to flame, IF(The Knifemaker bears his wife's passing, the story is her silhouette scored through time, IF(The Knifemaker naps beside his grinding wheel, the story is the mirage of talent, IF(The Knifemaker slivers the moon, the story is the hollow-boned dervish of nighthawks, IF(The Knifemaker loves from afar, the story is the poetry of anonymous carvings, IF(The Knifemaker casts himself in iron, the story is the transformation between molds, IF(The Knifemaker blooms wings, the story is the invisible tethers of work, IF(The Knifemaker trembles with fear, the story is a fortress secreted with weapons, IF(The Knifemaker brims with shame, the story is the slice of the blade's mirror, IF(The Knifemaker wanders the desert, the story is three wishes & white sand speckled with blood, IF(The Knifemaker loses his mother, the story is the hard apprenticeship to the father, IF(The Knifemaker loses his father, the story is the spared rod of the mother, IF(The Knifemaker smells his cancer, the story is a still life of scalpels & black grape tumors, IF(The Knifemaker staggers directionless, the story is arrows scratched in trees, IF(The Knifemaker slaughters butterflies, the story is the stained glass aftermath, IF(The Knifemaker hermits in a cave, the story is un-recognized genius, IF(The Knifemaker forges a sword, the story is a change of degree, IF(The Knifemaker carves out his eyes, the story is a memory darkness cannot snuff, IF(The Knifemaker slumbers beneath fever trees, the story is the slashed ghosts of mosquito netting, IF(The Knifemaker prophecies truth, the story is exile in a land shadowed with blackbirds, IF(The Knifemaker begrudges his brother, the story is their locked struggle & woven bones whitening, IF(The Knifemaker dies in his sleep, the story is a dream of immortality, IF(The Knifemaker sacrifices his daughter, the story is the secret of her lost virginity, IF(The Knifemaker sires a jealous son, the story is the father's prized dagger, IF(The Knifemaker ascends to fame, the story is smoke consumed by gray sky, IF(The Knifemaker sunders his ribcage, the story is sunlight interrupting the hollow, IF(The Knifemaker pens the law, the story is a thousand retributions, IF(The Knifemaker tempers high carbon, the story is shattered into a fragmented text, IF(The Knifemaker scars his flesh, the story is told in the braille his lover traces, IF(The Knifemaker field-dresses the fox, the story is winter starvation, IF(The Knifemaker speaks in tongues, the story is the assassination of the unbeliever, IF(The Knifemaker inhales the dust of his labor, the story is vermiculate lungs, IF(The Knifemaker buries his knives, the story is the glimmering funeral procession, IF(The Knifemaker pegs his thoughts to the wall, the story is madness written on rags, IF(The Knifemaker blanks his steel, the story is outlined violence, IF(The Knifemaker slays his apprentice, the story is the replacement's suspicions, IF(The Knifemaker seduces his neighbor's wife, the story is stuttered shadows beneath the bedroom door, IF(The Knifemaker hammers Damascus steel, the story is the pattern language of water, IF(The Knifemaker dissects his heart, the story is doves birthed from the chambers, IF(The Knifemaker endures fifty plagues silently, the story is fifty silent prayers unanswered, the story is a parched earth mosaic & a handful of seed.)))

Lindsay Herko

The Leaping Triangles of Youth

Our same-sexed love lived in the leaping triangles of youth—witch-hat regimes that held our hearts captive through VHS tapes whose spools were coops of dust but told the story of young girls vaulting power over logs in the woods. Logs, things boys wouldn't let them play guns with. The girls overpowering the wood and putting it between their legs as broom, wood's skinniest form, made it resemble a rising of power boys would never recognize, allowing them to rise, rise, rise above the scratchy rash of dried leaves and the raisin tongues of prickly peers and the raw egg smell of the sea-level art kilns in the academy to the part of the air that carries dew like a ribbon, to the part of the tree where you can peek down and access the health of someone's scalp through the seams of their hair.

And when this movie eventually ended, we put the foundational ecstasy, the kind that exists before and without estrus, through our chins, reaching out to the static beard of the television screen. I wanted to make myself a house shingle of green, to find a girl who would understand why I wanted to smuggle a black cat on the flat path that was my chest under my shirt. Imbibing Scope did not procure her. The mirror is an echolalia of the divisive experience of trying to break into the TV.

You tried to be a rigid airborne A, jumping legs in an unbreakable triangle, chances brighter if under an afternoon that showed a crescent moon, your crotch always broke and your knees always buckled and there should have been no hope had we not moved across our youth school like sickle cells in its arteries carrying the consolation prize twins of construction paper witch hats to consummate the primordial marriage of children checked out of their gender, possessing an other in a tunnel-private vision quest to obtain and parcel out snack time nutrients of power.

Our same-sexed love lived in the leaping triangles of youth—eye-touring the triangle windows in the stained glass gleanery on the front of small, summer-town churches, the presbytery stashed between the unlived lands and the marina of a two-hotel town with three old houses and a trailer park of summer people, the perpetual puberty of the Thousand Islands. The first rite of the fragile act of possession is to take the bride/bridegroom friend (adaptogen for friend—goon) through an expanding geometry of your own metaphysical loneliness. Take him or her to the places your parents make you leave town for, the ruralities where only one family lives all year. Take them to the unmowed graves of settlers who settled nothing. Take them to the site of a discarded and cross-fruit cocktail can left in a roadside gully bound for the hidden folk of molesters and the copulance of bees and exert pride that neither of you has to see this discard alone. Our Peter Pan and Peter Pan Peanut Butter Marriage undoes itself in the hues of youth, saving each night from suffocation as we hit the visiting the lonely-place pillows and had the benefit of lifting that can up to knife the twilight, our circle motions cutting a door knob to pull beauty out of an incomprehensible space no young one should process alone. Our same-sexed love can tour the cabin land churches, resenting the ones that smell reedy behind their triangle windows like the last century's dead, and we can walk gallantly in front of others if being in concert gives us each the confidence of being both woman and man, us together acting as auctioneers of the event of our non-marriage and our future marriageability to these teething but barely respirating spaces.

Our same-sexed love lived in the leaping triangles of youth—the tri-aggressive angles of girl friendship. As we caught ourselves lively in the apprenticeship of a devotion that would teach us how to later love another of the opposite sex—a kismet wrenching together of duos as pleasurable and powerful since the days of Anne and Diana, my Anne and I barely had time for the Prince Edward Island novelitas to cover our witch idols with their dresses before a third duck glided down with the intentions of polyamory.

We contended with jealousy but did not get distracted as we built the prism points of wooden boats to row our own rivers, as we made quiet observances in the heat-capturing conics of the wooden playground's highly spiritual "second floor," as we sometimes shaped a tired pile of fruit in our mouth on a low moment—like being almost quiet while our parents had audience with their friends at Niagara Falls within a restaurant called The Love Boat—making the fruit rise like a pyramid under the hood of our higher, inner mouth. Grapefruit held under the humming of Jonah and the Whale (differentiations taught by two churches), side-by-side of one another, as the adults passed lobster so charming it should have been wearing bracelets and we looked in silent recognition through the tourist trap porthole windows onto a clique of 35-dollar-a-night motel rooms with Canadian rainbows painted on the window shades. Indian immigrants in yellow sarongs followed the shades down, passing window after window, hoping to see the real rainbow in the belly of the Falls.

You, Anne Marino, were born a boar in 1983, a year for curly hair and the reddening of the inner folds—a throat naughtied from screaming parental politics were unfair, an ear heated with war against nickel when being pierced and getting cheap follow-up earrings from the zoo on the good idea they were zebras on metal-ball backs, a permanent blush behind the knee to only be caught by those kneeling behind you in gym class, tying a shoe, who happened to be looking. You were born in a dog bed of curtained anger. You were combed and shouldered caped in Burano lace and afflicted for licking yourself in a looking glass haunted for other qualms. You wore a velvet bib as the mirror colored your aura in medicinal ginger. You were born to guise Cranberry Pond—a crater of water in the outer curds of Rochester, New York—to a lens maker and nurse's household where sexuality would always confront you via oversized neighborhood rabbits that would come from their cages to gauntlet-offer sex to your bewildered family dog.

You tore up the construction paper waddles of an Easter duck with good dental care drawn by Jessica "Snow Bunny" Erwin in the concealment of being young—second grade, with the hot-water knives of your nut-colored eyes under the rare Italian green eyes of a teacher who wouldn't suspect you as she was too psychically preoccupied with enjoying a second wooing from her husband, who intuited she was going to have an aneurysm. You tore these things up in flagrant spirit because you dreamt Jessica Erwin knew you at home, even though you never gave her your address.

Jessica Erwin in her home-sewn animal print pants—black long leggings with brown geese flocking around the pleats—drew in your doorway while you slept, your curly head the top of a family tree—the insult of the tree being a conifer with two baby Asian heads, branches beneath you and your eyes, frozen to look doelike, unbecoming of your beloved role of foe finder general. You woke, angry that Jessica Erwin knew the secret of your adopted siblings and the failed seedlings your parents put down into the Earth, angrier that your tree was bushier than her eyebrow in evergreen roughness.

I was gestated into the last plates of 1982 after the laundry-cleaning event of my Yugoslavian great grandmother being put into a coffin in a November that felt strangely like summer, but by my December I was born out of the ground-absorb of the snow among the artificial lights of hospital that spoke of equatorial, middle-earth islands and the hopeful citrus spray of Metamucil caught in the gum of nurses who brought the sensibility of church to work every day. I was born while my mother could yawn and be girded by forceps. I was followed by a talisman of my mother's poop like a spine pointing to my head on the bed as my shoulders accidentally first clipped cotton, fomenting my lifelong curse of constipation.

I thought if I offered you the chance to see me walk naked through a room, I would somehow shed that curse. You did not want to see my attempt to not be ashamed by the smells that would later depart from me on road trips to Myrtle Beach in cell-sized bathrooms where shaving cream lay stagnant in the sink and other people's ideas of studs waited in long lines outside the doors and flies threatened to seep into my braids as I tried to pass a parcel of myself into the plumbing of Pennsylvania, to succeed at our game of challenges that included trying a seafood sub and drinking so much water, knowing that just touching the ocean would unlatch our bladders into peeing toward the sand. I never wanted to see you naked and worried in retrograde each time you told me of the Christinas of youth—a time when I instead was best-friending with rocky creek banks—of meeting girls who would ask you to play in their bedrooms only lying down, playing games of getting calm by letting your nose grow cold touching the sheets on the bed while they tried to quick-change beside you, hoping they would get a pelvic charge if you gave them a secret sign that you knew how they were taking advantage of you. Still you often slipped off your underwear under dresses in public places to wing it in a ring against the helplessness of our post-industrial city, or slipped your bathing drawers under the black of the Carolina ocean, becoming part of the great biological call of the universe, the parted leg, where nobody could see you, perhaps carrying clams within you back to our hotel room but always resetting yourself to a safer representation in the future, assuring me you would be you, lipping a sun-burnt can of Coke by the summer colonies where cemeteries also made up the small population of county residents and nights expected us to exist past tall days of evergreens vying for the attention of God against our small awkwardnesses, trying not to be part of their fight or distract with tossed panties.

I was not a gay womanist. I was a girl who was a boy in a past life. I was born in this life by sex, assumedly, in Larkin's Crossing, the first neighborhood of my parents for baby-making, though they had watched a cat fall into the swirling waters of a toilet in Arizona and fought black widows with hairspray while parenting my dad's older bulimic sister who also wanted to escape west. Maybe I was made on the energy of a steak sandwich and a rose-colored-lipstick-mixed-into-drinking-water—or worse, -milk—dinner system. Still I was born ready to build wooden coffins with you for our fantasies that fell away on the bridge of a hundred pre-teen to pre-twenties nights into days in a small clot of land called Western New York, middle-school Spanish coinciding with our first trips as private drivers up the oldest roads in our state towards Niagara Falls would teach me to call it "Nuevo York."

I did not know the date for sacrificial magic. I made the girl called Anne play flute on the night hill. I sacrificed her forever by making her a separate mind in front of a boy.

Next to her house on Frisbee Hill, the resilient playground never curved its wooden shoulders in alarm when plastic tongues of youth-fiber slides attached to their outposts, never cried to hear a mother swear on the phone to her editor for not getting an article on Clinton agendas with Russia done for a local paper while taking her children to play when others were in summer school.

The hill was full of pits we would not cross, filled under the dwindle-knots of weeds with the gossamer of life-reflecting mirrors buried there by aliens. Some of us grew up hoping to think of such things, watching Tarkovsky's *Stalker*, but the reality was our little Frisbee Hill that wispily looked at the sky, wishing it could hear Jewish folk tales rather than being round land incarnate. I made her walk among the pits in a long black skirt that would forever fit, as hers was not the type of life to grow fat at any later stage, and I made her play at the childhood orgasm of culmination in having one's own picnic for a first beau in celebration of his birthday, reaching the childish edge of crudity, carving an adult instigation. It was night—I had to be sorry and sheepish and borrow her mother's dishes. We had some sort of food I do not remember and tea that came up the hill made by the mother that made her. I brought a telescope that was too heavy to lift to see the skies. I had a curfew brought on by the chilliest part of early night. I made her play before the vocal concert given by the boy who liked her—a Michael who seemed more like a eunuch in a Vietnamese family of techno-skaters, endorsing the endorphins of their sexlessness as I burgeoned my own manliness by doing a gesture against my scalene attributed sexual nature with someone with the last name of Merkel.

She played her instrument as the dark reduced me to the thin straps of a rose-colored tank top, giving orders and pinning her before her admirer who dimmed to a smile, respirating lovelorn peppermints as he stood pigeon-toed—bracing against the wind, waiting for his falsetto—and embarrassed her.

I lost her. I sent them both away when the wind changed and there was hope it would blow the shyness of personally held hormones, cupped under arm and between lip and chin, through the boy-girl boundary of hill tabletop candles. Though there would not be much picnic time left to get a first kiss when leaning over roots under the blanket to pass a glass of tea made out of a jar—the clouds were balding, the moon bearing a choke-shawl of cold—there was even less time if I took moments to customarily imagine her whereabouts, her and him stumbling down the track-path riddled with pine, she separating the way while he fumbled with his silver music stand that could have done the work.

I sent her away.

She, me, now the equal but distant angles of an isosceles, from then on looking upward to the pinnacle-part of a boy who always gave us the connected distance to relate to each other. I still had all of her mother's dishes, but for the first time her 100-year-old house was hermetically sealed. She toothbrushed the contempt for me, for the first time brushing in concert with her parents, all of them going to bed at the same time like in days before I ever happened.

Matthew Mahaney

from *The Boys in the Trees*

On the hottest days, the boys in the trees peel leaves. You wouldn't think a leaf could be peeled, but they use their teeth and move just slow enough. Inside every leaf is a hexagon the color of cobwebs. The boys in the trees wrap them around their knuckles like bandages and have a kind of happy seizure under the afternoon sun. They are so small afterward, little broken kites draped over every branch.

Two boys have trapped a bird at the bottom of a glass jar. The three of them are sitting on the lowest branch of a stout tree. When I get a little closer I see that it's not a tree at all, but a pile of fur coats on top of an old piano. The bird blurs its wings in short bursts. I'm wondering if I should try to steal the jar and set the bird free when I notice the boys staring at me as if I'm late for my own birthday party. It feels like thousands of spider eggs are hatching inside my arms. They look from me to the piano, back and forth, until their meaning is clear. I pull the bench out from under the piano and slide into the nearest fur coat.

The boys in the trees have been lining their branches with jars. What fills them is the color of pennies and rotten teeth. I watch them swim down to collect handfuls of dirt and grass as if they are sleepwalking, as if they are on a mission created by their leafy minds out of boredom. A mouse appears from beneath the smallest boy's collar. It runs down his arm and into the tall yellow grass along the river. The boys in the trees don't notice any of this. Their eyes are still closed, their hands still buried in the earth.

The boys in the trees have been descending again. Last night they left a message hidden in the body of a deer. I found it on its side, curled tight around the trunk of an ancient pine. Its stomach was swollen with mice. Some of them woke when my flashlight hit and their pink little legs started kicking. If my wife were here, she would ask me why I keep going back to the forest, why I think a dead animal means something more. But I know what I saw. I know what direction the mice were headed.

The way they sit on their branches makes me think the boys in the trees want me to start singing. So I do. I sing the first thing I think of. It's a Christmas carol. Silent Night. By the time I get to the second *night*, each of the boys has a jar in his lap. When I reach *all is bright*, I can hear dozens of metal lids being unscrewed. I don't know if this is a good thing or not, if I should stop singing or maybe change songs. I don't know what else I would sing. I don't know if I'm trying to keep them here or drive them away.

The boys in the trees wear eye patches over their mouths. Each boy has painted an eye on another's mouth, a small white circle around a smaller blue one. The pupil is the patch itself, unpainted and glinting in the sunlight. One of the boys has cut a hole in his eye patch. He sticks the tip of his tongue through the hole and withdraws it again, over and over. At night I hear the sound of his tongue scraping against the plastic until the rhythm sucks me underwater, into a place so small there is only room for this sound. I start to forget everything I know to make room for it, every face and phone number, every conversation I've ever had. I forget whether or not I like coconut, if I've ever seen the ocean. The forgetting takes most of the night. In the morning the only thing I'm sure of is that the boys in the trees are never coming down.

I venture out in the afternoon, once the boys in the trees have gone limp. The ground rings out like mating swans beneath my feet. Inevitably the clouds turn dark and the wind picks up. The trees shift their tenants into more comfortable positions. Soon their fingernails are full of bark and I am wishing my wife would come running over the hill in a purple coat. My compass tells me everything but what I want to know.

I cut leaves into the shape of a child with no mouth and pin them to my shirt. The mouse bones in my pocket kiss my fingertips for luck. Having taken these measures, I head for the deepest part of the forest, for the tallest tree. After an hour my eyes begin to hum. When I look up, each branch sags with the weight of a dozen boys and the secrets they keep locked tight beneath the bark.

It's cold outside. The boys in the trees have started losing their eyelashes. Sometimes I'll see one floating down to land on my shoulder. It feels like plastic. Soon there will be enough to cover the ground, and I will gather them to make a fire. By the time it stops burning, the eyelashes will have melted to make a new kind of night. By the time it stops burning, the boys in the trees will have all slipped away into the space between branches.

And Live in Iowa

Today I was told I have prostate cancer lol

My wife pronounced our marriage a joke for the past ten years lol

I have 17 dollars and 32 cents in my savings account as of five o'clock pm lol

Late for work today lol

A suicide in the subway lol

My addiction to pain killers prevents me from caring lol

History is a crime against forgetting, but my memory is shot already lol

Seven years without you lol

Please turn me into a block of salt lol

When Mozart was buried his three friends refused to walk any closer than the cemetery gates. It was raining and they didn't want to get wet lol

I buried my cat Biscuit in the backyard lol

My beloved cat Biscuit lol

O Biscuit my Biscuit lol

Whom they slew and hanged on a tree lol

Yesterday I declared myself personally bankrupt lol

Consider me corrupt, rotten, mean, useless, a human stain lol

I went hatless into the leaning rain lol

Bald at twenty-seven, hairless in northern winds lol

Plantar fasciitis. A severe case of. This is what she said to me lol

Thursday. We all know what that means lol

Vallejo wanted to die on a Thursday afternoon lol

I look out a window, trembling in fear lol

My skin is an underbelly. How remarkable its unhealthy pallor lol

Where did I park my car? I have no idea lol

What day of the week is this? Where am I? Whose apartment lol

Will you love me? No, she said, no, I can't possibly love you lol

1955–???? lol

Imagine Beethoven bound by an iron silence, yet composing those great cathedrals to Western music lol

The Righteous Brothers singing in holy anguish lol

Ice. That I slipped on lol

God why do you hate the old sycamore lol

I set fire to a house when I was eleven years old lol

I went to shake his hand just as he withdrew it back into his suit jacket pocket lol

I never learned calculus. I believe I have a learning disability, a useless limb set at an angle in the mind lol

I am Canadian and live in Iowa lol

She's pretty. In the mirror, I see the pocked surface of my face lol

I would give anything to know how to speak French lol

Can I help you lol

O dark dark dark amid the blaze of noon lol

At work I wear a nametag, a hat with a company logo on it, an apron lol

No one believes me when I tell them I am trying to be a better person lol

Nine times thrown into the ice water lol

Evicted for non-payment of rent lol

My mother, wasted, crawling on the front lawn, wearing a bathrobe and smoking a Swisher Sweet lol

I have an MFA. In poetry lol

Health care. I don't have any lol

Liar liar pants on fire! is what they chanted lol

Awake in a cathedral of holy anguish lol

Love is an imposter lol

Forgive me for I have sinned lol

When I first saw you I understood immediately how impossible it all is lol

Do you remember the first night of Shock and Awe lol

That dark pit and what was discovered there lol

There's no cat food in the house and my little cat is hungry lol

My dinner cools on the greasy hamper lol

Black purple bruises up and down both forearms lol

The tree falls in the forest lol

Where do you want this killing done lol

Because existence is a quality of that which is perfect lol

A downpour lol

At work I felt like I was on the verge of a seizure lol

Dilantin. Phenobarbital lol

I make the income of a teenager. I am fifty-seven lol

The disappearance of wooden barns in rural America lol

Pies and high-blood pressure, small lesions on my lips lol

A dream of cataracts lol

When it was time to go I got up and departed and no one called to
stop me lol

One looks at certain things as if in haze lol

Why is beauty the premise for unresolved sadness on my part lol

Matches but no smokes lol

My friend tells me he's finished his second novel. I haven't written
a word in years lol

Snow howls round the cornice of my dreams lol

The desiccated body of a gray squirrel found inside the sandbox lol

Toothache on my birthday. My gift to myself lol

How interminable these must seem to you lol

Usury blunteth the blade lol

A loud, ugly man shouting at his guests on his television program,
telling them to shut up, abusing them, bullying them. How pleased
they all look, how content in their hatred lol

Up the dry brindled hill lol

The chicken and other natural wonders lol

The vice grip of time lol

Not the ground of being but the ground of the ground of Being,
the place where guilt sets down like stone under desolate sky lol

Magiscroft where did you go lol

Future of wood-louse, future of human monster lol

Moving about in the world bearing a shield upon which the word
FEAR is blazoned on his left hand, WANT on his right lol

Old music, old books, old men looking for work lol

Worrying over a strange looking mole lol

To be nothing all my life lol

My love, your hatred lol

The four-hundred-page thesis I realize late one night is useless lol

Seven years to write. Eleven minutes to burn lol

Watching boxing all night on YouTube lol

The bullfight. The horses in the bullfight lol

They are outside our house at night, crawling in mud, wailing lol

The jackboots scissor in brilliant menace lol

A nightmarish town, even old folks menace lol

I sing alone in a house on fire lol

A dream of Main Street in distress and broken lol

Lish's advice: Leave Iowa. You've been punished enough lol

Shoved against your car, cuffed, lights flashing, cops yelling lol

I have no money, none. And I need medical care lol

It is the cruelty of the age that brings me down. The vile, incessant
heartlessness lol

I barely know you, yet you hate me enough that you would kill me
if you had a chance lol

You're not going to like the diagnosis *or* the prognosis, Mr. Cone lol

To rage for no reason in the storm on the heath lol

It shall not come nigh thee lol

O unfashionable rain lol

O Kenneth Koch and his *Sleeping with Women* lol

What if you have no family, no friends nearby when you die lol

These are people who died, died lol

Even my cats find me contemptible lol

The nature of failure is how-do-you-spell-your-name lol

In a blizzard, unshod feet lol

My need to go out on Halloween dressed as Joey Ramone lol

My several weeks of Latin at university which I tell everyone was
two years lol

In a display window, those old typewriters no one will ever buy lol

Awl, tug, sack, hammer, cat, anvil, boots, weights, shovel, rake, paint cans lol

Detritus from an unnamed life lol

Coughed blood into a silk handkerchief lol

Tuberculosis and the poetic imagination lol

Cats, proper burial of lol

The prayer unanswered is the wound unclosed lol

The problems of poetry are essentially the problems of prayer lol

My posture's slow curvature lol

Lear gone mad upon the heath lol

Oedipus made blind by his mother's broach pins lol

The state asylum seen from the low mountain in autumnal light lol

In the diner where you saw an old woman tuck in the tag of an old man's cardigan lol

What Robert Oppenheimer said he thought when he saw that first atomic cloud: I am become Death, the destroyer of worlds lol

I stand in aisle three while an idiot's song blares from above. There you find me weeping lol

The elevator opens. You hesitate. It closes. I am lifted away lol

Suddenly it occurs to me that I no longer know how to do long division lol

Scalpel, cheesecake, toupee lol

And then they were upon her lol

I have not even heard the mermaids singing each to each lol

Mystery, that is, language lol

The air seemed green. I couldn't swim the length of a bathtub lol

I'm tired. I mean it. I'm really, really tired lol

A special place for those who would condemn both the guilty and
the innocent lol

The antique tanks settle into the wild rose lol

An elite guard in fetish footwear lol

My hands shake this morning lol

Spitting blood into the sink after brushing my teeth lol

The realization that the coat I picked up for free doesn't fit me lol

A broken city, a cold city, a mattress on fire in the rain lol

The cold that is my body that is my mind that is an antler above
the fire lol

The usual unusual city lol

Nothing lol

Nothing lol

Nothing lol

Nothing lol

Nothing lol

Nothing lol

A nullity lol

Nothing lol

Eleuthera lol

Family Portrait with Two Dogs Bleeding lol

The Plesyre Barge lol

Least lol

A bridal shop in a town where my beat-up face reflected in glass is
the only thing approximately alive near the riding seas lol

My homeland, my prison, my permanent exile lol

I have become mine own widow lol

The empty high-school football stadium in December rain lol

All literature is pigshit lol

Stay with me lol

An insistent reluctance to leave lol

O unfashionable rain lol

O singular cot lol

O bells that toll for me lol

O stone and glass, parking lot, spire, shuffling masses lol

O bridge over river held to by winter's hard vice lol

O television jettisoned by curb lol

O singular blue sail lol

O moth of my heart, don't let me die alone lol

A Garnish

Peter wants to touch Paul's corpse. I know this because he asks me if I want to. He does this sometimes with barbeque.

He says, "Janet, what do you want for lunch?"

"Chicken salad," I say.

"Not barbeque?"

"Barbeque chicken."

"Not pork barbeque?"

"Pork barbeque," I say.

We're standing in Peter's garden. The garden is overgrown, and Paul died in it. I don't know how long ago.

"Touch him," Peter says, "Find out."

It's been Peter, me, and Paul for so long, I've often thought if there were no Paul, there'd be no Peter, and then there'd be no me. That's not true anymore.

"I don't want to touch Paul," I say, "You do."

It's nearing afternoon, and we should probably eat lunch soon. I leave Peter and Paul in the garden.

I'm slicing apples, thinking of a bed of lettuce, a garnish, paint thinner, when Peter calls me to the flowerbed.

Paul has rolled onto his side. He's muttering something. It sounds like *alls*, or *awls*, or *owls*.

"Something ought to be done with him," Peter says.

To ascertain what ought to be done, I have to look at Paul. A thing I've been avoiding.

Paul is wearing shorts, slippers, and a terrycloth robe. The robe is open. The daily *Tribune* is tucked under his left arm. The crossword is half done, though I imagine the answers are all wrong. One of Paul's eyes is missing. I used to think if I could see inside his head, I'd find a smaller, distorted version of myself sitting on a bed. Paul was obsessed with me.

"What happened to him?" I ask.

Peter says that's not the question.

Paul was the kind one, Peter the mean one. I had no time to guess which one I was. Perhaps I was the slow one, moving like a stutter through a room, throwing an elbow to a vase, a clock, a champagne flute. I had to break myself into a person.

"The question," Peter says, "is what happens next."

Sometimes I found Paul sitting cross-legged on the kitchen floor, fixing something I had broken.

"His kindness," Peter said, "was oppressive."

Peter and I were not so pretty and not so kind, and unlike Paul, the walking hello with nowhere to go, did not court attention.

"His fingertips ejaculate desperation," Peter said.

Things were compromised by his fixings, ended up resembling him. Cracks sealed in the vase. The flowers replaced. The pool of water sopped up. The wood floors unwarped. Whole rooms beamed ruthlessly, "I am!" The world burbled Paul's endless greetings, "Hello! Hello! I know you mean well!"

And me, moving back from him, wrathful as a whisper: "I do not. You are not. I am."

So, perhaps it would be best, as Peter suggests, to dig a hole and put Paul in it.

"Use this," he says and hands me a shovel. "And when you've finished, hit Paul in the face with it."

Paul often said he always liked me best, even if I always did what Peter said. But it's just like Paul to use the word *always* and smother my time in his sentiment.

American Folkways

Mason blade. Poovey hammer. Cleblum trinket. Holster britches.
Magger film and bleed. In the deep registers in the sip of evolu-
tionary gruel that is your advent dream. Your ill-will advected into
our domestic stint. In the sun's rising a plush of peasants. Their
joyful labor music. Their diseased simpering. The obsession in-
vested in those whom your respective genitalias have pursed
together a parting or a music. In Germanic shrouds the tadpole
pistons. In hermetic gourds the artificial seedlings tick fancy like,
as I said, a gruel pursuant to this claim, tiny claim, inscresant claim,
you really should comport yourself better according to the times
and human pricks, divested as they are into a dilatory recorder of
their own making, they form the mewl in their sound and bubble
image, their mouths Lord apples, their mouths bright aria clouds,
their mouths bum apples in the eye of sponder crow which is the
eye of liquid time which is the eye of a dursty pickling road which
has no eye like the neether eye its pilky feathers hothering there a
death to all mens. All it is decidedly plural.

A never before experienced humdrum past an itching powder for nostalgia. Deluded a godless scratch the other century I still think of as this century. I have been lopped off my life terrible and ensured to drop off at a singular pace called advantages and disadvantages. What eight things are visible in this room in the twilight are the eight things that will discompany me to the heavens. There is a material insistence that just won't coke out and let me be. It is not a can of coffee grounds it is not my book thresher it is not my miniature trailer on fire it is not my stealth mouse it is not my light bulb tool it is not my noose loom or god trowel or thimble function. The shoulder of the renewal guide is very small. First time I was threatened I crawled into poovey I emerged on the itinerant killing floor, the snouts of sheep, the cries of serfs, the brackishness overswooning all, atmospheric blood and real blood, not enough to specify the dark as category crone or category sacrosanct. Airy ary one upon yeen nose ere are one before aree were a bird in the airish scotch-irish spleen ary one left ary one one rarish kind aiming to air it out aree alight aight irsh tater in the ground. Stob blue many various hillsides hillfaces master pine does the master thorough tune inwhole. Spring yak palaver stob spring blue and pine pond and fine and beneath the notish of the spring-florn hatefuls. Girls willfull with long teeth and roses. Shush they will hear. Never have been your little bird and this don't mean I am now.

Brilliant inquiry allows hewn influx to acquiry into news. Perfect blackness soretuned and nickered. The inference is I am all about to die. Extend this bough into a new anatomy. Warsh the coaling flats with a giant hose. Portume my blanks. Drag the accoutery into the dumpslide. A mather-tail of my credo and pact and muerto drone. Drock-tail raven was eating a mess of greens. Whitetail deer do it inscription the bark do the ride wild fox inscription the bark? After lordy married a gross of them he found some sea to push their children into sea green and sainted with the deception of howl and show. This was a mythological affair. My childhood jester sucked on tiny trainlings of ants like temple seeds. I've got a home in glory land fence-looting and picket wings the jowls of my prettiest aunt all humped out beyond the blue. What I hear in your language is an insistence a paradraining sortie the pure similitude devoted first and now therefore devised to tout the chimes of our labor in the muzzled oven, attend me. Uncle Lordy, the narrow-clovened roadway. Satin made with his speckled eye and transforming face. He writ a song the pitchfork blues. He writ a song the habitants between heaving and dearth is where the parable

finds its ancient trim and grackle. These same orange roads, proph-
ecies, dense magi, a moment of victim, an urge and a pledge, the
fair carytid displayed on no tenable allowance, the solar honk of
the ill-forgotten.

The picaresque gloamship has been overtaken. Vulpine quasars tot shamelessly through the universe. The captives can only gaze into the emissive, insectoid eyes of their alien torturers. Outerspace contains no turkles and rarely ever did. The musical tones generated by their heliotropic speculums invoke an ancient netherspace, afore memory, untouched by gadgetry, untouched by the experiments of winespoon gods. The hearts of the captives are naked. We fly, aglasmiated, toward the edge of dust. Inside the bellies of the aliens are lots of other tiny, pucker-mouthed aliens. I withdraw from the bridge and suck for a long time on my nebula.

Ranked habit aboard multifacent mysterio lens fractual seeing. Humours resin to thicket of gorge in throat and limbs. Flower mord or inseaming again, a prow, the lingering of deer on cosm, head of lance, escaped lunar prick, steroidial amaze. Sleet pilk on his head. I accuse the night of forfeting its graft. A nourishment of infinite languor is not in the stars in the fall ochre. The porch overwine the adjacent trailer houses with outed windows rote hollering a veritable assemblage uncoined of children and dogs and tires, to tell what from what, the propose of ownership vanishes in the colding musk and disturbs my solitary feud. Aright the feudal mastery and impress it on these. Blast of treacle, apparent mill spawn, a colonial model of instigation, so as not to own the pot pissed in so as not to murder the outhouse blues as the coyote murders sleep the river's slug dowry unpsent. Withstand the lattice its literal instance. Crush up any pill just crush it up into an anser a night disclined. Potter's field of stobs and pansies. Beheaded runnion head in poke and flung into the mulching pond. Nakedly as aught things are as aught but they are reckoned through the filters wrought from the devolution of rabid pack creatures into fortresses and men. Release the pardon pitched and message the unverse and the ones that followed their gangly respects and dark stovepipe hats their shredded calendars that slag into progressively greater and greater sleeps until the shape of the moon fills the trailer the moon itself fills the trailer. Dusk-harvest the green bodies and bottles. I am torn to dears. a rind in couplet, a spuming fontanel. In adversity demise. In fairest glory demise.

For the laggard totes the water and extinguishes himself. For the spatial dimension is not a bluebird. For the inoculation hath persuaded me. For a fragment of wolf-face lends the autumn its teeth. For the Cloud-King's aperture is also my aperture. For exiled from the votaries I sleep upon the tarmac. For the schizoid paramour does not make the bed. For excessive gesturing renounces the nightmare. For madrigals are not birds. For martens are my horoscope. For the flowers smell better inside her mouth. For she is a pauper and the abyss is damp. For the half-lit dining room is a cruel mechanism. For her estuary mouth and her wood of the dead. For the Lord is the Lord and her breasts are her breasts. For I am demeaned by sunlight. For the black poppy is a lonesome friend. For her hair is a thicket not easily deciphered. For a song is enclosed inside this thrappling. For a song is a borrowed peacock eye. For to undulate is a rarefied motion. For the farmers laugh at my rickety plow. For when people say "that's lyrical" they mean that words have been made to mean what they do not mean. For I do not live on a farm. For the shoat will shriek for its mother. For the Lord's ass is blue when his blue ass is on fire. For the burden of feeling does not save a fly. For the fondling of parchment is not an achievement. For the possibility of error inflames the satyrist. For the demiurge's blossoms are mostly contagion. For nothing more should be mentioned of her red chemise. For the ripe secret pours its blood. For I will not open a curtain during the gunmetal alarms. For the Lord is a little song and I am a little mouse and my mother is a little mote and beyond that I do not know. For the celestial brightness is shorn of its frame. For the frame is more important than the hands of a ghost. For the radiance of the winding-sheet is my radiance. For the clump of beans on the stove resists the Heavens. For she was not persuaded by my delirious horse. For the shadow expelled by the dark lung lies in the dustcart. For the typology of the ancients results in sad fucking. For my fork is missing one of its tines. For a sow is a plug of milkable time.

Emma Sovich

from *The Binding of the Body*

She skins herself. She will face the stars open, they will burn her a new skin. The old skin she soaks in lye then scrapes then pickles. It gleams on a rack. She can see herself in it. She takes the skin and stitches it to her waxen self. A shell shed for reuse, redefinition. An enclosure.

She bleeds over the old skin, the new not yet formed. Annoints, annoys, a noise. A flicker.

A bone in hand with pressure a friction. The bone of a swamp god, butchered, still tics. The bone polished polishes. She pushes the bone into skin into wax, gentles the bone along curves of lachrima, glabella, orbital. The bone still tics.

The bone chatters along skin and revises her template her. Pressure a fiction.

With enough pressure the bone will snap. With little the chatter louder, the ticcing pathological.

Her arm an array of muscles imbalancing.

Who Will Benefit from the Use of It

For the state's record, I spent my formative years in a tree, and then I went down the ladder into a dim beach shed where a man fed and clothed me. We had fine conversations until I learned to speak and he ran out of things to say.

"I'm hungry," I said. "We need root vegetables. Perhaps some turnips for our nourishment."

The man was not a good cook. He was not a close listener. He turned into wood. I hoped he would at least be a useful type of wood. Through experimentation, I found the density of his wood could withstand multiple assaults from a fast-moving steel ball. At its fastest, the ball traveled up to a speed of 100 mph before it marred the wood's surface. I spent many weeks observing the wood's eventual destruction. The results were not what I had hoped for. Finally, I abandoned my wishes and burned his wood for warmth and wept fat silvery tears that fell into the curling black ashes of his papery decay.

One day, a small ship approached the beach. It bobbed indecisively like a child's toy. When it came ashore, some men carried me up the deck and strapped me into a single-arm chaise lounge. From this vantage point, I watched both shed and tree recede into a surprising lucidity.

For a long time now, I have considered myself disposable.

Robert Lopez

How to Live What to Do

At night over dinner we look at each other. Someone says please pass the potatoes and we pass that person potatoes. We enjoy our potatoes but we never talk about them. They are potatoes. We discuss the day's events if there were any, if we can remember. Too many of our days are eventless, so most often there is nothing to discuss. We look at each other and eat our potatoes and wait until everyone is finished.

We're certain the weather is the same. The sun continues to rise and set at the appropriate times. There is wind and rain and snow and hail. There are seasons.

We don't know who we're looking at over dinner, which is why we spend time looking. We think it's important to look.

We still go to work, we have jobs. Crops are tended. Basic social services, shops, schools have all maintained regular business hours.

The people around the table can be anyone in the world though this is not likely. We're pretty sure people around the world have stayed put.

Sometimes we think we recognize someone, a grown woman, a young boy, a gesture or expression, a hairstyle.

Everyone has theories but the theories don't amount to anything, don't explain what's happened, not entirely. What we know is something happened and now no one remembers anything anymore. That's all anyone can say with certainty. We try not to talk about it over dinner.

It's not entirely true that no one remembers anything. We can remember certain things, certain functions and responsibilities. There is for instance a team that handles heating and cooling.

The temperature is never agreeable here and we think this has always been the case. It is always too hot or too cold.

Some of us seem smarter than others. Some of us are more assertive.

We tend to listen to the smart and assertive ones.

Most of the men have beards. Most of these are long.

The women all look tired. They all look like they need to go to bed and stay there until a better time.

We have meetings where we discuss new theories for how to live, new protocols for what to do. It is important everyone attends the meetings and for the most part everyone does.

We try to rotate who runs the meetings, meaning who has the gavel and who says things like the motion carries and the meeting is adjourned. No one likes this responsibility.

How to Live What to Do is written on a sign that hangs in the auditorium where we have the meetings. We hand out leaflets with *How to Live What to Do* emblazoned across the cover.

In these we have all kinds of instructions, from how to make pancakes to what to do in the event of a fire.

I am probably the best at running the meetings. I keep things moving and can run through an entire agenda in no time at all. The secret is not letting anyone else talk.

Only one time did someone object, and the issue was decided without incident. The person who objected was a red-headed man who had a disagreeable way about him. He seemed the sort that would argue with anyone over anything. I'm sure he doesn't enjoy the potatoes, for instance. He probably whines about having to eat potatoes every night for dinner. He probably wishes for turnips or carrots and complains about this at the table and everyone wants to bash his head in for him because of it.

He said something like I object to the way this meeting is being conducted.

I said overruled and moved onto new business. I think it had to do with transportation policy.

We don't think we had these kinds of meetings before, but we have them now.

Now people go outside into the weather and forget to put on clothes. What you see is women in nightgowns, men in pajamas, walking to the mailbox or putting out the garbage. Some are naked even. Whenever we see a naked person we are supposed to bring them a coat, take them inside.

Some people think it's the water. They think they remember a story about a company upriver. Others think it's because of the power lines or the power plant or that it's gotten into the potatoes somehow. We used to think we heard planes at night, so maybe it was the government.

There is one group, neighbors, who seem to remember what's happened, why things are the way they are now, but they're not talking. They never attend the meetings. Sometimes we discuss the neighbors over dinner and at the meetings. We don't know what's wrong with them or what's right or why they won't talk. Whenever we pass them in the halls they make a strange sound like a hiss. They never look us in the eye.

Part of the problem is we can't remember what the neighbors were like before or even if they were here before. We don't recognize them, but we don't recognize ourselves either.

What we do now is if you can't find your way home by 8 p.m. you can go into any apartment and spend the night. Most people don't sleep in the same place two nights in a row, we think, though we're not sure if this is actually true.

What happens is you go into an apartment and say I'm home and whoever is in there welcomes you as though you are family, which could very well be the case. Everyone spends a minute or so hugging and kissing everyone else.

We ask how was your day and we answer the best we can.

Sometimes we pour drinks for each other. We drink everything straight. No one remembers how to mix a drink and we can't find any books to help us out in this area.

According to the mailboxes a lot of us have three names, meaning first names, middle names, and last names. Sometimes the middle names sound like last names and could be maiden names if such is the case. We think almost everyone here is married, has a family. All of us have agreed to act accordingly.

There is one apartment, the neighbors', that's marked with a special flag so that everyone knows not to go there. Once in a while some of us forget and are expelled.

Apparently the neighbors do this without rancor.

The neighbors weren't a part of this particular evening so they didn't concern us too much.

Every day at work they have us go into one of the rooms with a blackboard and every day there is something new written on it. We take our seats and look at the board. Our seats are the ones you find in most classrooms with a desk designed for right-handed people. We aren't allowed to speak to each other while we are in the room. We aren't allowed to look at each other.

This is why we try to look at each other at the dinner table.

They give us thirty minutes to look at the board. They have us think directly onto the legal pads sitting atop our desks. We think like this for the allotted time and then are dismissed. Most often they shuffle us to a different room with a different board and we have to think about what's written on this one. We never see the other teams shuffling into the rooms we were just in, but we know there are other teams. They tell us how the other team thought better than us last week. Sometimes they tell us the score, how much we lost by. It's always embarrassing to hear the results like this.

Some of us think the neighbors are members of the other teams. This is one working theory, probably the most credible, but it doesn't explain everything.

In every room there is a sofa pushed back against the back wall. We never look at the sofa but they tell us before each session that the body is back there if we want. They say it exactly like that. The body is back there if you want. They don't say what we might want the body for and we've never heard anyone ask. During quiet time when the lights are off and we rest our heads on the desks, sometimes some of us go over to the sofa. We don't know what goes on because we are resting our heads, of course, but we know the body is back there on the sofa against the wall and we hear some of us going to the back of the room.

Today the body had fallen from the sofa and landed on the carpet, but the neighbors couldn't hear that. The body landed softly, like it had been laid down on a soft surface, like it was a baby put to bed.

It's not as if the neighbors don't make any noise themselves. Yesterday one of them was trudging back and forth in high-heeled shoes. We listened to the high-heeled shoes and imagined what it would be like to walk in them. We're not allowed high-heeled shoes at work so we can't say for sure.

We knocked on the ceiling with a broom handle and they knocked back. The knocking went on for about twenty minutes.

At night over dinner we sometimes discuss what goes on at work if we can remember. We never talk about the body at dinner. They told us this. They said never talk about the body at dinner or with anyone who is not a colleague. Furthermore they said never talk about the body with a colleague either.

I myself have never gone to the back of the room. I do think about it sometimes though.

As such there is almost nothing to talk about during dinner. This is when we try to play a game of charades or some other group activity. Sometimes it's cards, sometimes it's stories. Sometimes we tell each other stories. No one likes the responsibility but some of us think it's important.

Even if I were to go to the back of the room I'm not sure what I'd do with the body if anything.

One of us starts with something we can't understand, something about car mechanics. You aren't supposed to ask questions until after the story so we sit there and listen. One of us says we aren't certain what car mechanics do, but we're sure they wake up early in the morning to do it.

The person telling the story is a woman of indeterminate age. She has a prominent nose and it does something to her voice. She sounds like a cartoon character. She is wearing a brassiere over her sweater. You see this sometimes. It only looks wrong to some of us. We've been told we shouldn't correct each other unless someone is in danger.

Then she says something about the car mechanic's hands. She says they've been through a lot, that they need a rest.

Sometimes we let the children go off and play outside because they don't know any better.

The children are never allowed in the meetings.

We were at our window once watching the children in the street. They were having a game of touch football. We could see the breath coming out of their mouths because of how cold it was out there. The thermometer said it was ten below zero. I thought for a minute that it might be dangerous for the children to be out in this kind of weather but I think I decided the fresh air would do them good.

One of them went out for a pass and kept on going until she was out of sight. It probably took a good ten or fifteen seconds for her to disappear into the dark night. She wasn't a fast runner but none of the children seem especially athletic. We assumed the one who disappeared would find a place to spend the night. This is when we told the remaining children to come inside so they could get ready for bed.

First we had to run their hands under hot water so they could regain feeling, so they could brush their teeth.

We told them they played great, that they were all wonderful players. We asked what happened to the one who went out for the long pass and didn't come back. They said she was supposed to run a fly pattern but got confused. Then they said it looked like she went beautiful and they were right, she did.

Because I can remember this sort of thing people listen to what I say.

I'm certain this helps no one.

Most of us wanted to go back to our own rooms or whatever rooms we would settle on later once the body was on the floor like this as it was late in the day. Most of us were tired and had to get up tomorrow. Not everyone has to get up for work everyday but everyone said they did this time. The truth is most of us don't have to report in most days. Some of us stay in our rooms and do god knows what.

Sometimes over dinner we discuss what life must've been like before. Almost all of us talk about going back to our own people, finding them somehow. The children ask questions but we don't answer them. We tell them to go outside and play.

We're almost sure that we all have our own families. It's not that we don't regard each other as family, as our people, but we think we have other people elsewhere too, in the other apartments.

We wish them well when we can, when we can remember. We raise a glass and say something nice.

When the children go to bed you're left with your spouse for the evening. This is who you go to bed with and who you'll wake up next to in the morning. You are expected to conduct yourself accordingly.

So far we haven't had a problem in this regard.

That night in bed I turned to the person next to me and said it looked like she went beautiful. The person next to me said what is that and I answered it was what the children said about the child who went out for a pass but didn't come back. I said I liked the way it sounded. I said it might be the answer to what's happened to everyone. The person next to me didn't know what I was talking about, didn't remember anyone saying anything.

Then we made love.

It seemed fine.

In the morning, over breakfast, neither of us said anything about anything. We didn't talk about the children or anyone looking like they'd gone beautiful or our lovemaking or the body at work.

As we were eating breakfast I saw three naked people walking down the street.

Even this body, the one that fell, we were almost certain had other people elsewhere too.

We think the ones who don't have to report in are the ones who go to the back of the room to play with the body. At least this is one working theory.

It is all very experimental what goes on at work. It probably makes sense to someone somewhere.

But I think to those people it probably looks like all of us go beautiful.

We weren't sure who was responsible for the body falling on the floor. Any number of us had been near the body at some point but there was no way to tell who was responsible.

None of us ever point fingers.

It was suggested we draw lots to see who would take the body away so this is what we did. The process was equitable and went off without incident. One of us with soft-soled shoes drew the body lot and this signaled the end of the workday.

Everyone was then reminded of the neighbors. We were told to be mindful of the neighbors on the way out.

We didn't discuss the body or who it was that had to take the body away. This person, he had curly red hair and a beard. I remember someone telling him that red-headed people were being phased out. I remember him looking confused and angry.

He said what does that mean and someone said it has to do with evolution. He asked what is evolution and someone answered it's a theory.

Three of us were charged with helping him load the body into a wheelbarrow. All kinds of equipment are kept in the basement at work including four wheelbarrows. We don't usually have occasion to use the wheelbarrows.

As we were on our way out we all blended into each other, one body into the next, arms and legs, hands and heads.

Everyone whispered that it was a good work day in spite of the body falling like that.

This is when I stopped the one with the red hair and beard and pulled him aside. We let everyone else file past us. I held his arm and told him to hang on. The body was tied down into the wheelbarrow with twine so it wouldn't fall out.

No one gave us a second look. When everyone was gone I said to him listen. This is also when I told him he was being phased out.

After some back and forth I asked him where he was going to take the body.

He said he couldn't tell me that so I asked him why not. He said he didn't know.

I told him I had an idea but he didn't want to hear it. He said exactly that, I don't want to hear it.

This is when I hit him in the head with a lunchbox.

The lunchbox is made of hard plastic and makes for an effective weapon.

He fell straight to the ground as I don't think he was expecting to get hit like that. This is when I started kicking him until he lost consciousness.

Here's what's interesting, I have no idea why I did this.

I didn't have anything against this man, even though he did have red hair.

And I don't remember ever beating anyone up before. I don't think I've ever been prone to violence, if I had to guess.

I took the wheelbarrow and wheeled it to the other side of town. I didn't know what I was going to do once I'd gotten there, but I thought this was a good place to take the body.

I remember feeling a certain exhilaration wheeling the body away. I remember running very fast. I don't think anyone saw me and even if they did no one would know what to make of it.

I was a blur.

I'm sure it looked like I'd gone beautiful.

It felt better than making love to the last ten or twenty spouses I've had.

When I'd left him the red-headed man was still unconscious. I thought maybe I should try to resuscitate him but I couldn't remember how that was supposed to work.

It is one of the things printed up in the leaflets, how to resuscitate people.

If anyone asks I will say he was phased out.

I remembered that we had a meeting scheduled for that evening so that's where I went when I was finished.

I arrived a few minutes late and the meeting was already in session.

We don't call anyone by name at the meetings or anywhere else for that matter even though there are those names on some of the mailboxes. We use terms of endearment most of the time like sweetheart and lovely. During this particular meeting someone suggested that we pick out names from the mailboxes and adopt them as our own, that it would be more civilized this way. The person who suggested this said we could wear name-tags, as it doesn't seem likely that any of us will remember our own names anyway. But none of us thought this was a good idea.

So what we said was sweetheart, we don't think this is a good idea. Someone called out I second the motion and all in favor say aye so almost all of us said aye. There were only one or two nay-sayers so the motion carried. Then someone banged the gavel and called meeting adjourned and we all stood up and filed out into the hallway where everyone kissed everyone else goodbye.

Benjamin Clemenzi-Allen

from *A Seeson in Heckk*

PREFAST

a longg time ago,
if i i i i i re-membr, lif

waz a feast
of hearts,
acttual hearts opned

lik flowrs
tht burnd th rooff
of my mouuth in pattrns.

& Beautyy, that sweet hyena
recntly releasd
frm th braces on hr teth,

fell into my lif
lik leaves,

& lingrd a momnt
to mak me lov hr.

Bt thn sh lft me
alonee   to wallw in my shooes.

My cityy drownd in popppies
typsy on theirr own red
vrson of th sunn.

Hr fac & bust crownd

w/ idiotic laughtr, 1 foot
out th door, sh blubbrd

int my mouuth, a glass of mudd
in hr raisd hnd lik wine,

"am i a treasur to u?"

III. DELARIUM II

Anyy othr Tuesdday
(Aa tail of my own follies.)

i wak agin to night,
swallw a gollup of poisn-
perfume to killl
my mourning breath. Nble ambitins!

thn start by imaging some meate: a stak,
harrdning. The lil soggiest sndwiche
sitin on a woodn staire. Ths, & my Alcheemy of curds.

Bt i remaiin practicl: My shoes com offf
& go bck on. Eithr fooot,
it dosen't mattr.
Both hve hols.

& thesee othr wys i com undon:

1) whn walkking on watr, i always slipp.

2) night.

3) my teth are blisters on my heavng tongu.

4.) i swallw car prts too mke my engin go. a carburatr,

a pedl. i go!

ahead & hav my nap

in a bthtub ful of brokn mirrror glss.

refreshd, i wakke. Th lite & i in piecs, hair partd

on th right. i go ahd & bburn mor

famly picturs on th camping stov.

Ennuii, fruiit flies, mossy pils of porny bbooks-

thez othr wayz to com undone-

bt i reman practicl! Th trafffic stps,

& strts; my shoees,

thn i - fuckk - forgt my nam for good, godbye.

& screm th wrd 'ddeath' into th wintr,

mak it ice i'll rubb against my nippls

whle lokking thru yor windw;

or explor yur trsh to tast th spoilt turkey roastt
u kickd goodbye.

Th shadows of crmbs spilt across my lockless kys.
Th wrds 'knif' & 'hoppe' spelt acrost my lockless kys.
Th sknny antts, theirr nests - bbuilt bhind my lockless kys.

Eat anothr bullt
to hld stll
ths vertgo in my dizy bblood?

i tak mysfl anthr note insteadd to staay ths stupd stomch pain:

Dnt remmbr ham & peas.
Dnt rmmbr bread in choc sauz.
Dnt rmbr sun flwr sds.
Dnt los alll yur teth
upon yur path to Heckk.

III. DELIRIAA I

(Wiffe of a Husband, Foolish Virggin, Me.)

Deaar Muse, ourr saffe word isnt love.
Th sky turns
drk, bendds down
& crawls acrss
th pointd roofs of our cityy.

U mak me say, 'lov,' 'lovv,' 'luv'
'llov,' 'luve,' 'love,' 'luv,' 'lovvv,'
'luvv,' 'luve,' & fll my mouuth w/ poisn.

ghost of my rdemption, hauntr of my hair,
spiritt in tht forst of gravs sittng greazy behnd my earr,

i wak again to midnite.

Th flowr bush u plantd in my arm
drinkks only watr frm a fatt srringe.
Th ros bussh in my arm, its rootts & thrns
crampd arnd my muscls.
th ros bsh in my ar - its bbuds
spilll frm my pors.

i wak again to midnit
th stars pisss mor yellw snlight int myy narrw skll,
ths mannequin's hollw bbody proppd besid me.

i turn & tak my owwn hand agan in ths awfull drk,
thn stumbl arund th prk.
Ths height of minne, thes legs-
a surprse companion tht stayys beneatth me,
as i staggr on th flor.

Muz, i eat my cherios alon
w/ th moon, & starv.

Bt if i plac my severd arm upn ur wonky altr,
wrst plantd in the drt, fingrs feeling twrd th sky,

wil u tk hold? & pll a anothr me, plz, from

th rolling lloam? Stannd hm up, oyl hs parts,

& let him bloww out th lghts in myy own clinkin eyez.

I. BADDD BLOD

(Tear out th florboarrds & tile th forrest.)

fr my fauther, Bert.

Yur headd iss a crckd statue achng in plac of my skul

i become my fathr again. Bert. BK, NY, wobblng.
wearrng my ppr Crown, askin th st. signs & treez,
pleez, fr some hlp. I'm thiis woozzy low-wtt lghtnng bolt,

fallen frm th damp & dandrough sky,
no shoees on my ft.
th bar brnch heavy on th horizn.

Watch me wtch myslf being u, Fathr - living? SSuking air,
pizzza sauc drping from my palm. Ths isn't the wy u wnted to leav me

33yrs ago, rightt? It's wintr.
Th cold's a speare splittn my sidde.

i spk all nite int ths rustd mail box, 'dear me, u, & me - der u, me,
& U - dr fathr, son, & whtevr:
th famly busynes suxxx:

th messags, the endurring pain'
i m us again, Brt - absorbeing so mucch sleet - weezing
   around Bed-Sty
& leanning hngrey on this tre,

th emptty pizaa box of my palm -
opn, & those lst wrds u left for me lingrng:

"Take him: my son! He'll die instead."

viii: FARWELL

Farwell autmn. Farewl clovers. Farrwell cutt grass lwn, peach pitts. Ffarewell ssticks. Deatth, u filtthy memory wiped awy by age, Farwll. Farrwell vessels fluttering in nite belw. Farewwll nightt & dawn, duplictous coupl well known as sistrs eacch telling hr tail, their friendley hnds in combat. Farrwell beacch coverd in raggs & breaad & mourning breeze, farewell morning breeze, u pale angle. Frwell teetth fallin lik rain. Frwll nthing in th shappe of a gunn. U in th hat & clippd nails, u in th wintr snow, far-wel. Farwll shades of pigmnt on heavy breastts. Crampd aprtment on Central Blvrd, wher i bedded alon, & togther, farwell - livrwursst & onionss in red saucce, steam agnst my window. Farwll frankk & beans, & shoees full of my ft. Fawell basball clubb on my browning yrd. Faredwell yardsale; i cn see th orangg grov. Farwll organns & eys tht blistr on my brain. Farwelt

Far-wall

Far-wall

Far-wll

Farwl

Farwll

Frwll

& It Rains

There is a planet only populated by the emotions you did not speak, where the ocean holds continents with both arms & is fully aware of its actions. Yes, what I feed is what grows / yes, for two weeks, I only sit still by staying in motion. Your twin brother tells me nightmares are purification. My ex tells me I showed up in his dream & told him to look at the leaves. The psychic tells me we're at a fork in the road. A stranger tells me all roads lead to god. But nobody can tell me what roads lead to the roads: why the men that lodge inside me like a second spine can't identify my heart on a map, why the reality I create in you can lightning me with compliments & attraction but you can't say, as I tell you I'm disappearing, a single thing I'd have you say.

Jump/Push

A ceiling panel falls in the grocery store three feet from our heads /
yes everything is an omen. Let me start over: there's no such thing
as starting over. Since everything is everything, nothing is also eve-
rything. Yesterday a butterfly landed on my chest & stayed there
for a good thirty seconds & a month ago you lay in my bed & said
whatever you needed to say, & afterwards, when you apologized,
you asked if it brought us closer as friends. This butterfly is a
minister of apocalypse / I mean that with a whole shot of hope,
something stronger for a chaser. I've never been one to sit still. I'm
asking when the fuck do we get some electric wings? How do I see
the forest for all the cliffs? If all we've been promised is the mean-
time. If the meantime is the whole time. If the person you are to me
cannot remain the person you are to me.

Joseph Aguilar

Five Meadows

1

What's the digit. What's black and. How many sidecar. Why did the herbicide. What has fuss, a trill. Why did she prairie. How did. Why did she hi-fi. What did he give. How do you tell. What's the digit between two. Why doglegs, why chime. How do drunken. What's red and. What did the chimera. Why did the tumor in the digit. How many dead. Why can't. Why don't. How do we find.

2

Suppose middle names. Inter under beds or. Dizzy pretty mothers or. Snatch momentous news to. Calculate our groins. Well bolt cinnamon and. Go under the dock. Well lumen the moon or. Spindle water through. Turn the lawn then. Shrink into trees. And barbeque the pet.

3

Wheels beat mud. Can wheels churn balm up or. Gentle air down. Your fear hypostatized. What eats skin. To yellow rut. Months blanch all. The finer bones. Why are you crying. Over a hole. You owe all the. You you give. Can ants hole or hew. Can shade slay. Or ever flare the. Fire wet of yesterday.

4

To handicap a handicap. To paste a factor. To factor a landlady. To likeness a shallow. To shallow a nightshirt. To dashboard a wader. To wader a gobbet. To plantation an earpiece. To earpiece a handicap. To tenpin a handicap.

5

Propose midriff nappies. Hidden under cars or. Wobble prickled motors or. Whimper celebrated newspaperman to. Reckon our grounds. Well bomber nutmeg and. Charge under the doctrine. Well lurch the mop or. Spiral waterproof through. Roll the layette then. Fall into trends. And sauté the gold.

Eleanor Perry

from *Molt*

1

nimphe (13C), from Latin *nympha*, from the Greek *nymphe*: bride, young wife, veiled; related to *nubere*: to wed, to marry (see *nuptial*); a minor female nature deity in Greek mythology eg. *Lotis*, daughter of Poseidon and Nereus (see also *Lotis*: species of coccinellidae or lady beetles).

body wryxled a

persephonic clack

and thrum

threads wintering

in yolk-like

viscerasures

thrips of glyph

gelid the

epitheliad a

larval joke

jejunum

or a swell

where no

such

naked

is

2

larva: the immature, wingless stage of growth in insects, from the Latin *larva*: ghost-like, masked; *coleoptera*: beetle, from the Greek *koleos* meaning *sheath*; *flammeum* (from the Latin *flammeum*: fiery red) a Roman bridal veil of red or orange veil worn to protect them from evil spirits; *the lifting of the veil*: part of the ancient wedding ritual representing the groom taking possession of his wife as property; *exuvia*: the molted exoskeleton of an insect, from the Latin *exuo*: to undress.

chrysal is eggmass

a nailpolish sclera-thick of

eidola white neon

oil-smize dazzle

limbic where sun fretwork

evaporate like me-thing like jellyfish the

lost lacewing mine shrilly

fray

I, all that the bright lick of white

and so on

3

instar: a postembryonic stage between molts in certain insect species; to stud, as with stars; to make a star of, from Latin *instar*: form, likeness, image, resemblance; *Betelgeuse*: Alpha Orionis, centre of the Winter Hexagon, eighth brightest star in the night sky; in Lacandon, a Mayan language: *chäk tulix: the red butterfly.*

lookdown through

quark-soup sky

the bloodslug straggle

glasma haloes seeming

in the glister

a zygote in the star is blown

REFRACTAL

i like that it ghouls sterile like neutrino

glowworming

4

Ancient Greek word for butterfly: ψυχή (psyche), goddess of the soul, wife of Eros, god of love; also mind, spirit, breath, life. In Aztec mythology, *Itzpapalotl* (an obsidian butterfly) is a skeletal goddess with knife-tipped wings, ruler over the spirits of women who have died in childbirth.

hummingbirds with hi-fi skulls
flockblossom orizaba dark
to Coldharbour brick block   sky is trauma now
gin bruise and

                                    methancholia

abbatoir café eclipse and pisco gloam

          ooplasm cocktails the tangles of toiletgarble
          cough lingua

          SEVER at brixton

          flyover spraypaint

          nineties bitch
          so happy in the brain coral

5

coleoptera: beetle, from the greek *pteron* meaning *wing*; Ancient
Egyptian beetle hieroglyph: *xpr* or *hpr* or *kpr* – to transform, to
come into being, to become, to emerge; Plutarch: *"[this] race of
beetles has no female"*; the male sacred scarab, thought to repro-
duce by ejaculating into a ball of dung, an act of self-creation
resembling sun god *Khepri*, said to create himself from nothing.

slocked i am

discoslither

quirking in the

gleed of

old shitball

gimmicks o

godgasm auric

in subway

sheeling i don't

like the *slick*

                    of

The Games They Played

BUTCHERSHOP

Because the older was the butcher and the younger the pig. At least that was how the older explained it later, when the mother found the younger laid out across her best platter, stuck and sorry. While the mother and the older argued, the younger moaned through an apple, said some words lost to worms. In a rage the mother removed the open knife from the younger's side and when her rage did not subside she stabbed the knife into the older's heart. In the minutes that followed, it was only the older who died, clutching his chest on the kitchen floor. The younger escaped unscathed, despite the platter pooled with his blood, because when he received his wound it had been only a game.

PIPER

Because the older always played the piper, the younger had to dance before her, learning the jig and the jitterbug and other dances too, flapping her skirts and kicking her feet up past her knees endlessly and for hours, until at last her breath broke and her ankles trembled and she collapsed to the playroom floor, almost-almost reenacting *the night of the exhausted and dying dancers*, the tragedy that gave their play its other name. By this foolishness the younger wore out another pair of shoes every other week, so that their soon-penniless mother had to beat her into stillness, while in the other room the impatient older waited, demanding, instrument in hand, ready to resume the measure.

HORSE

Because the older was bigger first, when they played *horse* he was the horse, the younger the rider. The older's role in the game was to wear the bit and the bridle—a wood dowel with two holes drilled in its ends, through which was looped a braid of twine—and then to allow the younger to ride him bareback through the house, the yard, the first few feet of woods, whinnying and bucking and galloping all the while. But *younger* did not always mean *smaller*, and as the younger grew so did his burden, so did his anger that his horse could not carry him faster. As adults, the older's bent back was no longer strong enough to bear his bowlegged brother, but by then the bit and the bridle had worn a deep and permanent smile into the older's lips and cheeks, a reminder of the joyful days they'd shared as children.

CAGE

Because their favorite game was cage, and in this game the younger and the older took turns locking each other into pantries and cupboards, wells and grates and chests and other tight spaces. The tighter the better, they cried, the tightest the best. The younger especially excelled at finding new and smaller cages, but as the older grew it became harder for her to play along, to play the prisoner's part. Still the younger pressed in upon the older with her hands, fitting her new breasts and hips into the iron square of the oven, the porcelain squat of the teapot, even the tiny gold heart of a locket, given to the daughters on the dawn of their mother's disappearance. Only later, after the older was vanished too, did the younger at last remember this littlest detail, so long ago forgotten: It was the mother who had taught them *cage*, and before her disappearance it had been her favorite game as well, and before her, the mother's own sister's. And what was inside the mother's locket? With no one left to squeeze her bones, the younger never found out, but by then the older knew: Not a wood but a woodlet. Not a house but a housette. Not a family but a famliken, tiny folk with tiny games, little rules all their own.

You Must Have Felt the Dead

will and the way
his heart swelled

lick of his scarf
across your face

when he pressed it to his face

if not for those points
of leakage

there could have been
a marriage

replete replete
with packaging

what is that hovering

it looks like a husband
look how it tingles

at the head
confusion at the roots

how they playfully interchange
with the hawks

good in a way

like a small grassy knoll
where your fingers are

I'm never fully sure

N. Michelle AuBuchon

Haircut

After the girls died, my wife and I developed a routine. It started out simply enough. We ate dinner, which usually consisted of a casserole or something with chicken brought by loved ones: chicken French, coconut chicken, chicken tzatziki, chicken and rice, chicken everything, all of it tasting the same and the two of us just staring off from an empty table and chewing, because we were told that would help, the eating, but the only thing that actually helped was locking ourselves up inside the girls' room, looking at a portrait Lakshmi drew of herself and her younger sister, Dahlia, and knowing all day at work that after eight hours or sometimes nine hours of hunching over, pretending, you would come home and lock the bedroom door and act as if the doorbell was not ringing with the next day's chicken and hold your wife's hands and go so deep inside looking that it would slightly resemble something you once referred to casually as living.

Dahlia looks down in the portrait on the wall. She's picking at her fingers. She was always looking at her hands, Dahlia. "Try to look around you," my wife would say. Dahlia would look up, but her eyes were somewhere else, and her left one naturally wandered, as if it were trying to escape her body entirely.

Lakshmi protects our sweet Dahlia. Her right hand rests on the front of Dahlia's shoulder, the left hand extends around her back to cup the waist, holding and bracing. A tidal wave hangs above their heads where they stand on the shores of the Arabian Sea. The paper is tacked to the wall with a red push pin.

This was all part of the routine: looking at the picture on the wall with the red push pin after eating the chicken, sometimes holding hands and taking turns getting up from Lakshmi's bed to get a better look, pressing a clammy hand to a paper face. Going to bed, going to work, counting the minutes until the sitting and the pressing and the tidal wave was the thing you were doing again.

A certain night I took too long, hours perhaps, standing, looking at Lakshmi, her eyes swallowing up all the parts of me interested in hurting. I felt my breath slow then disappear, a memory of breathing and being and looking at Lakshmi— dissimilar, really, to living inside a drawing, but we don't mind it. It's just that our mother needed a haircut and I intended to give her one. Father looked so sad standing in front of us, his skin falling off his face, the flesh just hanging, whatever still lived inside of him mute and indeterminate. Mother, on the other hand, looked dead, and all I could think to do to help her was give her a goddamned haircut.

I took too long looking that night and my wife said, "Sit down for a bit and let someone else have a turn." And I don't know which part was Lakshmi and which part was me, but two hands pushed Mother down on the bed, and I said, "It's time someone gave you a haircut," my right hand pinning my wife's shoulder down on the bed, the left hand cupped beneath her back, protecting her. I think she screamed. I had the feeling of remembering being scared of her, that woman, my wife, but then I just got to wanting to cut Mother's hair, and I said, "Hold still, Mother, these scissors are sharp." But before that Father ran into the kitchen.

"I'm going to get the good scissors," he said. And then Mother, all dead and vacant looking, got up from my bed and came up to Dahlia and pressed on her. And then Mother's left eye started spinning around in her head like a top, and all of the sudden she got to looking not so dead. And that's when Father came back in the room and pushed Dahlia down on the bed.

Mother said, "Stop it, you're scaring me."

Father said, "Dahlia would do what Lakshmi says."

Dahlia said, "Just go slowly."

And then I said, "Hold still, Mother, these scissors are sharp," and that's how the whole routine got more complicated.

In terms of the haircut, I got the right side trimmed up nice and was getting ready to start in on the left when the doorbell started ringing. My wife said, "Don't stop." And then she just kept screaming, "Don't stop, don't stop, don't stop," so I took off my pants and really got to pressing into her and cutting that hair until there was hardly anything left. But poor Dahlia got scared afterwards, screaming about wanting all of her hair back. I am better at being a boy than my sister.

Anyway, today I came home from work and my wife was sitting in the kitchen. She hadn't warmed up any chicken, and she wouldn't come into the bedroom. She wouldn't even look at me, but Dahlia's eye was wandering, so I picked her up and just laid her down on Lakshmi's bed, and now I'm whispering into my sister's ear about who we were, my right hand resting on the front of her shoulder, the left hand extended around her back to cup the waist, holding and bracing, loving from inside this picture, before the tidal wave hits, just watching our parents lie there holding, whispering, pressing, unsure who is who and what is what.

Sara Veglahn

from *The Ladies*

We place our hands over our heads. We wave them back and forth. Our hems hang to the ground and become damp in the wet grass. Every morning it is the same. We must greet the new day thusly. We wave our bodies back and forth like seaweed.

Our bird calls have become more and more authentic. We have practiced for a long time in an effort to communicate with the chickadees, phoebes, finches and flickers. We speak to each other this way, too. The two-tone whistle of the chickadee serves as "where are you" and also "I am here." The frantic cadenza of the finch can mean many things. We have constructed entire paragraphs of dialogue from the song of the finch.

It is time to go to the river to make our offering. We do this each day. A pebble, a smooth bit of glass, a piece of bright wool. We toss these small objects into the river and concentrate very hard. Then we gather the water in buckets. We march back to town like children with our buckets splashing onto the sidewalk. We are children with buckets of water, we are whistling birds.

As girls, when the guns were put into our hands, we didn't want to. Holding a shotgun is hard. Heavy and cold and the recoil nearly knocked us over the first time we fired. Say "pull" and follow it and only shoot when you're sure. Pull and follow and shoot. We became good at it. Really good. We could see for miles. Our timing was impeccable. Our aim was precise. Everyone said we would clean up on the lakes. Ducks and geese. Blinds and boats. Early morning and too cold. Shooting trap was a game. Clay pigeons were not in the shape of flying birds but bright disks, like someone's idea of a bird who had never seen one.

Only once did we shoot to kill. Just to see. And then when we saw it, limp and heavy, we knew it was over. It was confusing to us that a tiny steel ball could end a life. What did it matter if there was something extra? With glass or clay it made sense: it shattered completely. It was so clear. But a body is different. Sometimes you can't even tell.

Now the dead are put into our hands and we don't want them. Holding a corpse is hard. Heavy and cold and we recoil from the stench. Say the words and sing and wail and howl and grieve for us, they say. Reach your hands up and don't let them take the coffin out of the house before you're finished. We became good at it. Really good. Everyone requests our presence. Everyone thinks we can help.

We often felt uneasy. Like a sliver beneath the skin. There but not.

We took the rocks from their holding place and placed them on our chests. The weight of them was comforting. They held us down, as if we would fly off without them holding us there, as if that were possible.

Summers, we would lay ourselves down in the creekbed and pretend we were minnows. We'd walk far into the valley and climb down where the water was shallow and clear. As we let it rush over us we tried to imagine the end of everything. The water would wash us away to the larger river and into the heavy mud that lingered there. That was as far as we could imagine going.

Eventually, our hunger would overtake us and we would emerge completely soaked, our hair streaming dark down our backs, our dresses clinging to our calves. But by the time we walked out of the valley, we were completely dry, as if it never happened.

Our hunger is insatiable. We find ourselves pining for all manner of foods: lamb and carrots and mushrooms and chicken and kale and mustard and ice cream and chocolate and paté and shrimp puffs and beef stew and rice and beans and escarole and noodles with curry and little crackers with cubes of cheese and various lettuces and other things we have never tasted.

Mostly we eat radishes. Like Rapunzel's mother, we pull the red globes out from other people's gardens. We eat them there, crouched over the green leaves, spitting off the dirt. We move from plot to plot in search of them. We wait until nightfall and creep slowly through the backyards.

If we were left, we were fortunate, although our fortune and our understanding of it weren't clear at the time. At the time, it was excruciating. We felt hollow and worn. We felt our hearts twisting in our chests. We felt blind, like pigs moving through sticky sludge. Our understanding was limited because everything we knew was veiled. It wasn't real. They told us the blue trees we said we saw appear in our bedroom, or the heavy winged thing that chattered around our heads late at night, or how the river spoke to us, clearly, in a language we knew, were nothing but lies. But even if we were the only ones to see blue trees and the flying animal flying around our heads and the only ones to hear the river speak, it was enough. We knew we weren't like the others. Always, we knew this. It was the way of the other world, to which we did not belong, and which, no matter how much we studied and observed and tried to learn, we would never really know. It was removed from us, it seemed. Forbidden. We were in between and would spend our nights weeping, waking with puffy faces, wondering why we had been so isolated, why it was us who couldn't take part, who could learn to be that way, who would never be admitted.

What we were thinking then was that we didn't actually exist. What we came to know is that we would exist forever.

Mere Increments

We have reached a certain point.

I am present. Mary has asked me a question, which I have not answered. We are in our bedroom, on the bed we share as a married couple, Relating. Our legs are individually crossed in a style that can be described and commonly understood as "Indian." Mary waits for me to answer. She leans slightly forward. Her earrings undulate in tiny arcs. They are small gold replicas of dolloped ice cream cones each struck through with a circumscribed slash. Her eucalyptus oil smells as strong when she is near to me as when she is not. Mary does not eat ice cream. She is anti- what comes from potentially farmable animals. Her hair is springy. It encompasses her head from the neck up.

"I'm fine," I say.

Mary's expression is concerned.

Our bedroom is on the second and most elevated floor of our house. It is a few simple strides down the hall from our children's rooms. Julie's walls are painted different bright colors: as I picture them I do not remember which wall is painted lime green and which is painted pink. Regardless one runs parallel to the other and those they intersect with are baby blue. There are posters hung of teen idols I know only by name. Julie and Edmund are both in there asleep. Cousin Chet's visit has disrupted the usual arrangement of things. It is something the kids have voiced their displeasure over. Chet is closer to me—Edmund's room is closer to me.

The north wall of our bedroom is double windowed and gives view to the Corn™ below us. This flicks and sways in the wind. It looks blue and dark and dramatic in the moonlight. During the day it is the vivid synthetic green of a John Deere. I can make out the massive, abiding rumble of the pumps as they feed the Rootz™ in the distance. This sound gets lost much of the time. We are just used to it, I guess, like we are used the notion of our need for vast systems of subterranean pumps to water our ailing Heartland™. It must produce somehow—what would we do with ourselves if the land did not produce? Would we be so different?

"Roger," Mary says.

This barely registers.

How do I—do I alone?—exist in relation to the corn-Corn™ differential? Am I multi-faceted in this way, this purely hypothetical way? The black plastic beads beneath our backyard's FieldTurf™ vs. the dirt my knees would collect as a boy? Am I defined by these implicit hypotheticals? This difference is outside of me. Indeterminate, poorly defined, I am the things I am not, though how can I be? I crave definition.

I sit at the head of our mattress. There are several throw pillows to each of my sides in addition to those we sleep on. They are red and gold and so match the room's overall color scheme. Mary picked this and I believe the eroticism I see in it was unintended. I rest my back against the oak headboard. The upstairs carpet is conspicuously off-white. My posture, I hope, is relaxed. Past Mary, on the east wall, is the entrance to our master bathroom. It is adjacent to the walk-in closet. There are papers in my hands.

I am okay.

Mary's expression signifies her desire that I would answer. What the question is is what was her question? Her face is an imperfect oval. It sits above her body like a distressed moon. A dimple exists in her left check that is absent from her right.

"I think," she says, "as though we aren't working on the same level. There's an underlying issue you aren't telling me. This inwardness, Roger, it's not healthy. Not for your Self or your relationships—our conjugal body, specifically. This fissure, sweet pea, emerging in our extra-corporeal oneness. Tell me what's up, or else, I—"

Mary's voice is thin to begin with and then dissipates. Her hands are tan and slender and marked with sunspots. The shape of them indisputably implies grace. She brings one hand to her mouth, and though it pains me, I am unable to muster adequate Relation. The Funk and its underlying Problem prevent it.

More of my papers are spread across the comforter between us, Mary and I. Most of these have at some point been drawn on, attempts to give shape to the factors that constitute my Self as they polydirectionally shift and I sense them shifting and am confounded by how I should justly communicate them to another who is not-me.

The papers in my hands are smeared with the pink and gray marks left from frequent erasing. Mary takes note of this. She types it into her log of Diagnostic Postulations (DP).

A numbness originates and lingers in my right leg, near the ankle, as my leg falls asleep. Mary cannot feel this. It occurs to me that one of her legs may also be asleep, or that both may be. I wonder if a breast can similarly fall asleep, or what it feels like for the female anatomy to become aroused. I wonder if all erections feel as mine do, if others identify the same hues by the same names as I do, if by observing Mary's "red" kimono I and another could agree not only on the name of this color but also on how it "physically looks" to us. I cannot think these things. They are at best pseudo-therapeutic, and even this, I think, is a stretch. I shift my weight to redistribute fluids. I uncross my legs and after some moments the numbness intensifies and goes away.

The thing is, I want to answer Mary. I love her deeply. It is obscene how much I love her. The extent of my love for her sometimes causes me physical pain. My stomach spins with the fury of a supernova, and inside of my body I imagine gigantic flashes and infinite depth that manages to somehow grow beyond its limitlessness and leave me with nothing, a vacuum. I do my best to honor her when she pleads that the construction of analyzable space for my emotions/self-concept is for my own benefit and will ultimately strengthen our Relation system, that providing mere cursory examinations and/or dismissive grunts is not only unhelpful but may actually harm the therapeutic arrangement we've thus far hammered out.

"I understand," Mary says, "that the consciousness and the body are separate entities. I understand that what's in front of you is merely a setting, and that your mind may be somewhere else, some other place at some other point in time, and that you may think differently of yourself in wherever this place is that you imagine than you do here. But please, Roger, you live within the conventional familial model. You have the kids, and you have me. Like the rest of us, you live inside the roaring tempest of globalization. You are not exempt. We're your fundamental responsibilities, us right here. Should we try another self-concept map? Rodgey. Let's get back to the basics, here, Smokey Bear. Let's chart something that locates you in this model so that you can understand your place and transcend it. Maybe then you'll tell me what's on your mind. Hm? Come on. No more straw men? Does that sound okay? Huh, Rodgey?"

Mary's pleas infiltrate me.

"Will you author yourself?" she says. Mary says this instead of "write it down." "Will you author yourself? Do you at this moment possess the ability to remain situated in such a way as to do this?" The question seems to occur inaudibly (though I swear I can hear it): "What's real: the body or the body of text?"

I set my papers down and pick at the cuticles of my fingers and get hung up on the hangnail chronically present on the outside of my right index finger, which is the finger I use when I am at my technically-oriented job at the Everett Paper Corporation (my title is Systems Analyst, I am a Systems Analyst, a serious Systems Analyst, I repeat this to myself frequently and silently, solemnly, Roger Jeffries Systems Analyst, fixated on systems despite the fact that I maintain and occasionally code them as opposed to mere troubleshooting, and in this way I encode myself in them, linguistically inseparable from my profession as if to form a single word, "rogerjeffriessystemsanalyst," a very particular and unhappy noun) to click the mouse attached to the company PC assigned to me. I bite the hangnail with my front teeth and press down on it with my left thumb. I strive for the words. I wish to answer Mary in the most simple and effective fashion. I pause as sometimes at work I analogously pause whatever activity I may be immersed in and identically fixate on this hangnail. I suspect that this may have to do with why I don't keep a nail clipper at my desk, not by the solar powered Queen Elizabeth II figurine given to me by several college pals as a gag gift before our (Mary's and mine, not my college friends' and mine) wedding, which rests next to the coffee mug I purchased myself that reads in block letters:

I LOVE MONDAYS...
(and then, revealed following a 180-degree rotation)
...ALMOST AS MUCH AS I LOVE MY BOSS

itself adjacent to and slightly behind the 1" deep HD computer monitor issued to me as well as several family photos from a distant vacation to the Wisconsin Dells: the monitor is framed in black plastic, the pictures in faux-gilded polyethylene, the white ceramic mug is the container for all of my pens and highlighters which I use to note and mark the various papers and manuals for the Objective-C programming language strewn across the surface of my desk—this all conceals the desktop calendar I rarely write anything on that has this one dog-eared corner that grates at me, and I figure as Mary leans even closer that I need to let go of this thread, it is a distraction from the Problem, I need to pick my battles—making my cubicle the kind of linguistic center of the Carroll, Iowa satellite office. My particular space fixes me via a set of flimsy gray partitions spatially in the center of the office suite and metaphysically in my professional duties, though I see how

Mary looks, and it is apparent that the hangnail only bothers me so much because it too is a distraction from the Problem. I am explicitly conscious of this line of thinking and withhold it for fear that Mary may properly identify it as mere free association and fundamentally pseudo-therapeutic, maybe even anti-therapeutic, though I cannot help its presence nor the illicit fact that I find it illuminating.

"I'm fine," I say, "Yes. That sounds good. I'm okay and well and whatnot. Mary?"

As I pinch my lips at their corners and feel the pressure contained therein even itself out across my mouth before it escapes and spills out and permeates the greater portion of my head's interior—in no way helped by the swaying and rocking motion my shoulders enact, or by the way my arm seems to automatically extend as I tilt and I am grasping for the nightstand, nearly knocking the smoldering stick of Nag Champa incense to the floor and in doing so causing a portion of the stick's low-hygroscopic resin to pool on the nightstand's surface, which dries quickly, the resin does, just in front of the lowly-lit bedside lamp—I display a facial expression that I believe to indicate my ability to maintain my cool, an expression that is intended to give off the impression of engagement while not positing any feelings of indifference or the many varieties of resentment that are possible, not unlike my professional veneer, and in this way it is a well-practiced look that

Mary consumes as what she observes certainly registers and she un-crosses her legs and thrusts her body at me from across the bed, causing her legs to go rapidly outward in a chain of motions that is so unified and elegant that the complexity behind it is submerged and the ornamental gold bangles around her right ankle clank together, the coup de grâce of her elongation and a sound I so tightly tie to her that I suspect I would conceive of her differently should it cease to exist. Mary's hand is on my shoulder. I have achieved a realization of my condition. My ignorance of the dual halves of our conjugal whole, of the world beyond this in-expensive sheetrock barricade, of where I can possibly stand, is heralded by a surge of fluids to my head, then blackness.

"I'm okay," I say.

I am alone.

We are in our kitchen.

The forms come into shape. I reach forward into relenting darkness. There is a hazy mound to each of my sides.

I reach out and brush one and observe its spongy feel.

The shapes congeal. I discern their names.

Bud and Mona Nord from across the street flank me at the dining table. They are each wearing a bathrobe and slippers. Bud's is a red-red ensemble while Mona's is pink-pink w/white pin-stripes. Her slippers are furry and mimic bunnies.

I cannot tell precisely why they are here—that it is for moral support is apparent, however they are practically strangers. There is something clinical about this arrangement. Mary could have called any one of the proximate couples along Qualcomm Avenue to the same or similar effect. For some reason she chose Bud and Mona Nord. Judging by their shallow systems of wrinkles and their easily disturbed temperaments, I estimate the Nords to be somewhere between 50 and 55 years of age. I often see Bud in his driveway spraying the side of his boat with a garden hose, or sitting in a lawn chair beneath the frame of his opened garage door looking out toward the street. He frequently parks his Nord Heating & Air Conditioning truck on the curb. He waves sometimes as I pull in. Mona I know less of.

Bud comments between scuttling laughter that he is grateful the table leaf is still in from the Mary-inspired and I would say self-aware FOURTH OF JULY HAPPY BIRTHDAY AMERICA BAR-B-QUE BASH, which was long enough ago that I can describe it as belonging to "last summer." It is apparent by the way Bud Nord brings it up—how this bash was so vast and delectable that he wonders how a woman who as a hard-and-fast principle refrains from the consumption of meat or any kind of animal product or byproduct whatsoever is such a wizard with the tongs, because he is still, he says, packed full and can use all the seating area he can get—that Mary's explicit point, the neighborhood outdoor barbecue "as object," was and still is lost on him. Mona gives no indication.

Mary approaches me with a Nestle Bottled Water Product she obtained from the 48-pack in the narrow pantry. The pantry stands next to our hulking brushed-steel fridge as though in meager parody. I at first intend to nurse the Water Product in a manner articulating gratitude, but instead I let it pour into my mouth, drinking it all in several large gulps. To my knowledge Bud and Mona Nord have never been past our foyer. Mary will not medicate me.

Mona, becurlered, says, "You have a lovely home, Roger. You and Mary must be very happy together. Bud and I have a lot of admiration for the life you two have here. We never had any children ourselves, you know. You wouldn't know that, I suppose, but we didn't. We tried for a lot of years, but it just never worked out how we intended. The technology just wasn't as good then. We've come to terms with it. We manage to stay interested, though, even without kids. There's nothing really at stake, I guess, except for how we feel about each other. Isn't that special? It's been a lot of work, I'll tell you what. I can't imagine what it's been like for you two. Mary tells us you have an extra one staying with you for the summer? He has an internship, I understand? We think that's just great. Monsanto is a very well known company. He sounds like a wonderful young man. I'm sure you were that same way when you were his age. What is he, anyway? 19? 20? I suppose maybe 21. Either way, it's ambitious what he's doing and quite admirable. He's probably all set to graduate soon. He goes to Iowa State, Mary tells us, and he wants to work in the CornFieldz™ as an agricultural engineer? I bet that's why he's here with you, is that he admires his uncle. I don't mean to gush or ramble or anything, Roger. Embarrassing you or getting on your nerves is about the last thing Bud and I want to do. We're just worried."

She curls her lips inward and pats me on the wrist.

My cigarette craving and the weird craning phenomena in my neck begin simultaneously as I notice that Mary has actually picked up a notepad and commenced jotting down my interactions with the Nords. Her red pen is ominous. I don't know exactly what she is writing. The window behind her is cracked open. The kitchen smells vaguely like fertilizer and acetone. The pumps are at work and there is the chirping of birds even at this hour. Mary looks at me and around me, at the two Nords and the objects separating us. The green tile of the floor and backsplash attempt feebly to simulate a more idyllic space. Mary is to my left. She stands out against the white lilting curtains decorating the window above the sink. I lace my fingers and pull away from Mona's grasp and place my hands on the table, palms down. I erect my spine, trending toward a question mark shape, and smile a smile that is not too big or small. I do not show my teeth.

"What's up, Rog?" Bud Nord rolls a jowl over his shoulder and back. His cheeks sag, O-mouthed. "Everything okay, buddy?"

Mona Nord scoots her chair back from the table and gets up out of it. She invites Mary to sit. As Mary takes her place at the table I notice a feeling of emptiness between my lips, a small circular area of negative feeling. Mary laces her own fingers as I have done and places her hands atop mine. Mona sits next to Bud. The Nords each face me. I feign ignorance of the shape my neck must be taking. A protuberance emerges on my neck's left side as the right slowly becomes caved in. I cannot speak. My smile grows despite me.

I consider my limbs. I have never come close to not having all of them. My limbs are my extremities. Mary's hands are clammy but still exude a kind of unpretentious glamour.

Her role in my decision to quit smoking, to "become" an ex-smoker, is complicated and not always pleasant.

"Roger," she says. She is not fucking around: I fear my smile has grown too large for its intended purpose and now appears exaggerated (possibly comical) and unconvincing. One of the several vertebrae pops near my skull, causing the Nords both to gasp, and Mary to scoot closer.

My neck is craning and causing my head to turn: the room itself appears as though it is turning.

A cigarette craving, I have noticed, typically will first manifest deep inside the torso. I think of smoking. A surge of serotonin from the GI tract and central nervous system. I feel as though there is one between my lips. The light thrown from the fixture above the table is yellow and seems to encone and alienate us from the relative darkness of the rest of the kitchen. I feel my hands begin to shake. I pull them from under Mary's and rest them in my lap. She breathes deeply and looks into my eyes. She is intense. I can feel a similar pressure emanating from the Nords. I rotate at the waist to look at them. White drooping jowls; I think I see tears in Mona's eyes.

It is not unheard of for an ex-smoker to feel like he has one between his lips even years after quitting, similar to a war veteran who has lost a limb and wakes up in a cold, sweaty flashback feeling as though it is still attached. I can perceive one dangling, the circular force acting in all directions on my lips. I can taste the rich, smooth flavor of roasted tobacco as an amputee can feel the cold sheets rub against his absent toes.

"Jesus, Roger," Bud says.

I calmly and with care reflect on a particular DP in which Mary and I discussed the nature of my nicotine cravings. I gather and internally recite the main points. A nicotine craving is physiological in nature and therefore can best be summarized as the internalization of external factors. It is derived from created conditions which are essentially corporate, thus rendering it a fundamentally orchestrated experience. The Self is in this way manipulated by indifferent or malicious factors, totally obscured. Mary's hand is once again on my shoulder. I can feel the air as it moves through my mouth and my lips begin to stick to my exposed incisors. The confusion produced by internalizing introduced factors hinders the process of Self-awareness and ultimately feeds the bottom line of the Problem. Mona's eyes definitely have tears in them. They are running down her face in thin rivulets that catch light from the ceiling fixture in certain spots and look kind of pretty. Mary's expression has hardened. I can see her simply by moving my eyes, though the angle is new. I cannot tell if I have not seen her wear this expression before or if it is an old expression seen simply from a new perspective. A soreness develops on each side of my head, right behind the ears where my jaw meets the rest of my skull. This feeling is more or less symmetrical. I do my best to keep a straight back. My hands rest in my lap. I am afraid that the indulgence of a nicotine craving would be the denial of Mary. I picture my briefcase leaning against the desk in my home office filled with things from work—the laptop they have issued to me, numerous papers and pages of object-oriented code seizing my admittedly very fragile and fractured attentions—and I realize I am in a way some kind of destroyer. It is evident to me that Mary desperately wants to understand my internal life, that she wants to experience it for herself in the most literal way available to her. This transcends words, I suspect, as her and the Nords' expressions do.

Mary wishes that we could mutually offer our essential Selves to produce something new and beautiful. Total Communication, as Mary has referred to it. She has told me this. This is all she has done, however. It is all she can do. All of our efforts to locate Me, to refine and essentialize my facets through processes that suggest some kind of Relation operating protocol, our agreed-upon "best practices"—to use a phrase I would never in my life utter out loud (despite the damned truth it invokes)—alter and create a new Self-concept that is removed from the one initially of concern, so that any move toward understanding terminates its referent through the use of "mere increments" and provides an ever more ruined simulation of the duplicate this "new" Self-concept succeeds. We destroy the Me she pursues and reproduce the process. It is not a game, I admit.

Mona starts to make these little whimpering sounds. Bud Nord's eyes become as large as the frames of his horn-rimmed glasses. The soreness behind my ears spreads both up and down. I can feel air flow across my gums and eyes. I can taste the atmospheric traces of fertilizer. Mary puts her arm around my shoulder with some added force. I notice, as the room turns very slowly sideways, that a small section of Bud Nord's 5 o'clock shadow is longer and bushier than the rest. Of course fear and self-consciousness have set in. I look about the room and breathe deeply and even though I can feel that my teeth separating and the words, "I am a complex and dynamic human being," beginning and continuing to issue from between them, I do my best to maintain an erect posture with a countenance I hope depicts an interested calm, though judging by the unanimous expressions of unmitigated terror around me it is evident that my face is not how I intend it to be, but rather it is some other way, some other combination of muscular flexions/contractions that has the corners of my lips turning more and more upward so that my transmitted words are distorted.

Bud Nord has resolved to call the proper authorities, which I assume to mean an ambulance and the precautionary squad car. With her foot Mary pushes the front-left leg of my chair so that we face each other. I look into her eyes. They are perpendicular to mine. Our points of reference form a coordinate plane. I love Mary and everything she wants from me. Though our DPs are nominally designed to retrieve Me from the Funk—a name Mary and I use for its irony, its quality of depicting my indefinite condition comically, that serves as a sign of our mutual hope that everything will be okay—and remove all obfuscating externalities, in practice these sessions serve to place me at the center of a very small and intimate realm and attempt to situate me as a being defined by my multiplex inner qualities. And so, I admit, as the angle of our eyes becomes more and more acute—I wonder if it will actually double back on top of itself, causing our eyes to share an angle though exist as inverses—my reasons for liking the DPs are many and ultimately selfish. The motivation behind my pleasure is, I am aware, grotesque. My upbringing rejects it. I feel embarrassed for enjoying something so mutually personal for such an infernal reason. I hate that Mary does not get to partake in the same way that I do, that the very act of Relation ends in widening the innate gap between us. My self-centeredness must be absolute. It is only me, just as it is only Mary, or Bud Nord, or Mona—though the latter, I observe in my verticalized periphery, has moved to be near her husband by the window as he describes this incident into his phone and now cries as he speaks loudly over my own embarrassing voice and listens—and the angle separating Mary's eyes from mine slowly closes. Mary reaches out and places her long fingers on my neck. She strokes and feels me as I crane and work to affect my practiced stoicism. The proliferating soreness is complicated and indistinct and in areas comes to feel numb, neither sore nor not-sore.

"Roger," Mary says.

The Nords huddle on the other side of the kitchen and dull their sounds for fear of waking the kids upstairs, though I hear the sirens wail much sooner than I expected as they exit the Pepsi Turnpike and speed down Qualcomm Avenue, which I imagine is lighting up house by house, and it is not long before Chet is in the doorframe by the foot of the stairs, and for his sake, as Bud Nord takes him into the living room to explain what is occurring, I attempt to stifle my words, "I am a complex and dynamic human being," which seem now to be something of a slogan, a coined term to be embedded in the memory, and likewise work to maintain my spine's failing posture twisting beneath Mary's soothing touch.

She speaks my name again as the sirens grow louder. Mona Nord goes upstairs to tend to Julie and Edmund. It is at this moment that the angle between Mary's eyes and mine aligns and we are viewing each other on an identical plane. I see her eyes and the way the capillaries in them form patterns. I focus on nothing else, and I can tell that she doesn't, either. She studies my eyes, too. The capillaries in Mary's eyes that I view and study with great care and attention swirl and branch and form webs that constellate. The room's temperature is slightly elevated even with the AC running. We just sit this way. As the ambulance arrives in our driveway and I hear the rehearsed, efficient clatter of the EMTs performing their protocols, I do not fear most the warped condition of my face or body or my speech as it continues to issue forth, "I am a complex and dynamic human being," nor the various tests and procedures that the medical professionals of the Hostess-Medtronic General Hospital will certainly conduct in the succeeding hours, but rather I fear the loss of this suspended moment when Mary's perfect stare meets mine, when I will be pulled away and become a patient transported and shuffled along and administered treatments according to sets of best industry practices that are optimally functional and cost-effective, attended to and eventually cured by a network of employees with varying skill sets and levels of education and professional ambitions who will each see me in some way as one unexceptional detail—another regurgitation of many prior patients—of a Sunday night's shift. Mary will pick me up after I have been cleared for my release. We will walk down the white lit hospital corridor each holding the other's hand as we approach the ER reception desk. The young woman sitting behind it will be humming along to the music playing from her headphones, and she will not lift her eyes as we move past her and the waiting area where others who are afflicted will sit and stir and we exit out the set of automatically sliding glass doors with the universally known neon imperative glowing above it. We will cross the parking lot to our white minivan in which we will drive home and we will sit together in the kitchen I am in to jointly discuss this instance and use it to Relate before retiring to bed where I will wake up tomorrow for work, and in this way I will be erased.

Jessica Richardson

Elimination Song

Ash berries pack in clusters like kittens or babies if kittens and babies came mewling from patches. Strong they sing, but even people sing strong now: sounds like *ah*.

I'm in a garden, so locate me that way. I've already grown arms, long ago. I've grown shoulders and fingers. I hope not, but I might have forgotten certain parts. I'm making up for this with my hands, which have minerals in them. I sprinkle dust on the dust, and do you know what? It sparkles.

I'm just as a fairy or something. It's not for lack of effort. I sing other things besides my own garden, but they are not mountains. I sing, for instance, beams. They've been lowered to the ground from an unknown structure. There's an unknown structure losing its beams, but do you know what? Sprinkle. Also, a tightly wrapped newspaper in a blue bag wastes under a bush.

What does the news have to do with ash?

I will look to history.

A decade ago I stood in the middle of a suburban street with five friends at sunrise and we tore a newspaper to shreds. We didn't plan it. It was as if we were animals, oh. We grew claws in sync, teeth.

We would no longer tolerate this terrible news, so we simply didn't. Shreds flew past the tiny pieces of wood and fluorescent plastic tape used to demarcate borders. *Here, I planted something*, the signs sing to the neighbors. *Keep out.* But the news shreds would not keep out because of our ripping and their falling. We felt hilarious.

This is what the news has to do with ash: no garden is impenetrable to shards or bags.

This is what the news has to do with ash: the stories that were falling, they were stories about falling.

Now, listen: I will attempt to strengthen ground as bone quivers, as thunder pops and moms lactate, and yet—how to sturdy the garden that reaches and reaches for more? We have this in common. Our fingers snap and dragon, pound. Beneath is never enough.

As if I'm an earnest waitress, I come and try to try to hear hunger, to take requests from this infested garden—a stand in for other things, like everything standing is. The plants, the berrying ash, my hands or my friends, they do not know what they want. Can we blame them? They think lyrics like push, exponentiate, push, kiss but are wrong, or sometimes are, or I'm lying that I know what they sing. I'm likely missing parts. Check off bodies, check off water, check off checking off. To find what is wanted.

Let's try a process of elimination.

C Dylan Bassett

from *Explanations of Blue*

(People in an empty house and mostly I don't know their faces. They never mention him by his real name. I keep the television on for the noise of it. Everyone has an idea, what he did, which medication, etc. Most people have been dead for a long time. Why bring it up again? It's easy to write the word.)

it's like the desire to be a soldier
to lose a war on purpose

home is impossible, he said
we can't even hear the hummingbirds

(I talk to him on the phone for an hour, then remember he's dead. A butterfly beats behind the curtain which is my face. Does loneliness make one more beautiful or less? In a dream he's walking away again. If he keeps walking he'll reach the water. Soon he reaches the water. Things will get darker before they get totally black. His jacket is black, his hair.)

when the wind wakes me it is for nothing

the blue is empty except for its sky

the lake, twice dead,
refuses to reflect a star

geese dive not knowing
the difference

once, alone in his bedroom, my father
insisted he saw

a deer stepping out of its skin

(A camera sees the subject unmoved. The subject is seen though a glass. A description of the subject's wet coat. A description of time. The subject has not moved. The police officer gestures a sinking ship. A description of hands not unlike a description of moths. A description of weather. The notable absence of snow. There is a stranger in the crowd who never speaks. The subject does not speak. The subject is lit by camera flash.)

dogs dig their way out, but never arrive

there is the mystery of a body buried
deep in my childhood
that I will never solve

there is the image of an entire family
who abandoned their house,
blankets still folded

real snow never falls
I paint the roof to look like snow

(A room flooded but no water. I wake up and wait for what. I count the aluminum sky in photographs. Death was a smaller story when I was young, a bed was called a bed and looked like one. On the radio they say winter is crossing the mountains. Whomever I dream is still alive.)

briefly I catch myself in the window
but no one's there to witness it

aspirin unravels in a glass of water
in which a ship begins to sink

is the rumor I tell myself

a prayer ends without
thunder

a paper dog runs from a paper fire

(I disguise him in the dream. A bear mask made from a paper plate. A crow speaks out of context, a mattress swings from a meathook. An ambulance spins on ice. He combs my hair with his glassy fingers. The sky is clean, the grass perfectly cut.)

so few days and thousands
of miles

almost nobody
is ready

I know the way home, or
I'm just walking

there's also the way a lake rises
taller than itself
the water churning

like insomnia

("Sometimes there was a blizzard. I was trying to escape the blizzard is one explanation.")

a bathtub overflows into the dream

words fall out of a sentence

was it an accident?

was it real?

I wear someone else's

clothes

a gunshot scatters

deer like blood

(At first you only see his finger. The whole body is always surprising. The fog kicks up as a plane begins its final descent. How much will the body change before it isn't his?)

the words come in whatever order

a telephone ringing but nobody

to answer it

when will I become invisible, he said

I said, people see each other everywhere

I saw a face in the bottom

of an empty bowl

I tapped it with a spoon

(Wind arrives from no direction. I see nothing I could show you. A ghost is in possession of a chair. A ghost smiles like a shotgun. In another version, I turn wind back into a word. I am toys bobbing in a swimming pool.)

things break because
I can't hold on to them

everything feels
the same except worse

tightly the earth
turns away

I am building
a ghost out of a body

Alan Sondheim

Back through awk

Every organism is an organism of and by slaughter, every landscape, a
landscape of death. Hannibal's elephants haunt the Alps. Where nothing
lives always has fuzzy boundaries where the limited exigencies of life are
contested. I think of the unholy matri-patrimony of aM and what it has led
to, almost a denial that only Rilke was capable of. Actually climbing to
the bluff, the church, the grave, seems an impossible memory now, as if I
have robbed the experience of another. Memories always teeter on the verge
of recognition.

Back through awk
```
{
for ( i = NF; i >= 1; i-- )
printf "%s ", $i;
printf "\n";
}
```

a landscape, every slaughter, by and of organism an is organism Every
nothing Where Alps. the haunt elephants Hannibal's death. of landscape

are life of exigencies limited the where boundaries fuzzy has always lives
led has it what and aM of matri-patrimony unholy the of think I contested.
to climbing Actually of. capable was Rilke only that denial a almost to,
I if as now, memory impossible an seems grave, the church, the bluff, the
verge the on teeter always Memories another. of experience the robbed have
recognition. of

Rev

a ,epacsdnal yreve ,rethguals yb dna fo msinagro na si msinagro yrevE
gnihton erehW .splA eht tnuah stnahpele s'labinnaH .htaed fo epacsdnal
era efil fo seicnegixe detimil eht erehw seiradnuob yzzuf sah syawla sevil
del sah ti tahw dna Ma fo ynomirtap-irtam ylohnu eht fo kniht I .detsetnoc
ot gnibmilc yllautcA .fo elbapac saw ekliR ylno taht lained a tsomla ,ot
I fi sa ,won yromem elbissopmi na smees ,evarg eht ,hcruhc eht ,ffulb eht
egrev eht no reteet syawla seiromeM .rehtona fo ecneirepxe eht debbor evah
.noitingocer fo

Tac through vi :g/ ^ /mo0

of recognition.
have robbed the experience of another. Memories always teeter on the verge
the bluff, the church, the grave, seems an impossible memory now, as if I

to, almost a denial that only Rilke was capable of. Actually climbing to

contested. I think of the unholy matri-patrimony of aM and what it has led

lives always has fuzzy boundaries where the limited exigencies of life are

landscape of death. Hannibal's elephants haunt the Alps. Where nothing

Every organism is an organism of and by slaughter, every landscape, a

tr A-Z a-z

every organism is an organism of and by slaughter, every landscape, a

landscape of death. hannibal's elephants haunt the alps. where nothing

lives always has fuzzy boundaries where the limited exigencies of life are

contested. i think of the unholy matri-patrimony of am and what it has led

to, almost a denial that only rilke was capable of. actually climbing to

the bluff, the church, the grave, seems an impossible memory now, as if i

have robbed the experience of another. memories always teeter on the verge

of recognition.

tr transposition

Evory orqknssm ss kn orqknssm op knn ly slkuqrtor, ovory lknnsmkpo, k

lknnsmkpo op noktr. Hknnslkl's oloprknts rkunt tro Alps. Wroro notrsnq

lsvos klwkys rks puzzy lounnkrsos wroro tro lsmston oxsqonmsos op lspo kro

montoston. I trsnk op tro unroly mktrs-pktrsmony op kM knn wrkt st rks lon

to, klmost k nonskl trkt only Rslko wks mkpkllo op. Amtuklly mlsmlsnq to

tro llupp, tro mrurmr, tro qrkvo, sooms kn smposssllo momory now, ks sp I
rkvo rollon tro oxporsonmo op knotror. Momorsos klwkys tootor on tro vorqo
op romoqnstson.

substitution

Evory orgonosm os on orgonosm of ond by slooghtor, ovory londscopo, o
londscopo of dooth. Honnobol's olophonts hoont tho Alps. Whoro nothong
lovos olwoys hos fozzy boondoroos whoro tho lomotod oxogoncoos of lofo oro
contostod. I thonk of tho onholy motro-potromony of oM ond whot ot hos lod
to, olmost o donool thot only Rolko wos copoblo of. Actoolly clombong to
tho bloff, tho chorch, tho grovo, sooms on ompossoblo momory now, os of I
hovo robbod tho oxporoonco of onothor. Momoroos olwoys tootor on tho vorgo
of rocognotoon.

Pig-Latin

Everyway organismway isway anway organismway ofway andway ybay
aughterslay, everyway andscapelay, away andscapelay ofway eathday.
Annibalhay'say elephantsway aunthay ethay Alpsway. Erewhay othingnay
iveslay alwaysway ashay uzzyfay oundariesbay erewhay ethay imitedlay
exigenciesway ofway ifelay areway ontestedcay. IWAY inkthay ofway ethay
unholyway atrimay-atrimonypay ofway aMway andway atwhay itway ashay edlay
otay, almostway away enialday atthay onlyway Ilkeray asway apablecay

ofway. Actuallyway imbingclay otay ethay uffblay, ethay urchchay, ethay avegray, eemssay anway impossibleway emorymay ownay, asway ifway IWAY avehay obbedray ethay experienceway ofway anotherway. Emoriesmay alwaysway eetertay onway ethay ergevay ofway ecognitionray.

Punched Cards

```
 _____
|  o     .o  o|
|  ooo  .oo  |
|  oo   .o  o|
|  ooo  .  o |
|  oooo.    o|
|    o   .   |
|  oo  o.ooo|
|  ooo  .  o |
|  oo   .ooo|
|  oo   .   o|
|  oo  o.oo  |
|  oo  o.   o|
|  ooo  .  oo|
|  oo  o.o  o|
|    o   .   |
|  oo  o.   o|
|  ooo  .  oo|
|    o   .   |
|  oo   .   o|
|  oo  o.oo  |
|    o   .   |
|  oo  o.ooo|
|  ooo  .  o |
|  oo   .ooo|
|  oo   .   o|
|  oo  o.oo  |
|  oo  o.   o|
|  ooo  .  oo|
|  oo  o.o  o|
|    o   .   |
|  oo  o.ooo|
|  oo   .oo  |
|    o   .   |
|  oo   .   o|
|  oo  o.oo  |
|  oo   .o  |
|    o   .   |
...
```

Eliminate

```perl
#!/usr/local/bin/perl5
while (<STDIN>) {
    @words = split /[\s]+/, $_;
    @spaces = split /[\S]+/, $_;
   for ($x=0; $x <= $#words; $x++) {
        $word_count{$words[$x]}++;
if ($word_count{$words[$x]} == 1) {print
$words[$x],$spaces[$x+1]}
        }
    }
```

Every organism is an of and by slaughter, every landscape, a landscape death. Hannibal's elephants haunt the Alps. Where nothing lives always has fuzzy boundaries where limited exigencies life are contested. I think unholy matri-patrimony aM what it led to, almost denial that only Rilke was capable of. Actually climbing to bluff, church, grave, seems impossible memory now, as if have robbed experience another. Memories teeter on verge recognition.

Elimx.pl
#!/usr/local/bin/perl5

```
while (<STDIN>) {
    @words = split /[\s]+/, $_;
    @spaces = split /[\S]+/, $_;
    for ($x=0; $x <= $#words; $x++) {
        $word_count{$words[$x]}++;
if ($word_count{$words[$x]} == 1)
    {print $words[$x],$spaces[$x+1],$words[$x-8],"\n"}
        }
    }
```

Every organism

organism of

is and

an by

of every

and landscape,

by a

slaughter, Every

every organism

landscape, is

a

an

landscape death.

death. elephants

Hannibal's haunt

elephants the

haunt Alps.

the Where

Alps. nothing

Where landscape

nothing

of

lives boundaries

always where

has the

fuzzy limited

boundaries exigencies

...

Mathesis


```
&parse_file_into_words("zz", 4000, " \$i/4 - 10 *
    sin(\$i * 20)"); sub parse_file_into_words
{
    print "\n";    #blank line
    my ($extract_filename, $iterations, $formula) = @_;
    open(IN,  "< $extract_filename")  or die("can't open
$extract_filename:
```

```perl
  $!");
  my $line, $i, $index;
  my $full_file = "";
  while ($line = <IN>)
  {
    chomp($line);
    $full_file = join " ", $full_file, $line;
  }
  close(IN);
  my @words = split(/\s+/, $full_file);
  for ($i=1; $i<=$iterations; $i++)
  {
    $index = word_index($i, $formula)-1;
    print "$words[$index] ";
  }
  print "\n";    #blank line
}
sub word_index
{
  my $ret_val;
  my ($i, $formula) = @_;
  $ret_val = eval($formula);
  return int $ret_val;
}
```

another. always organism slaughter, organism on another. recognition.
slaughter, every always the of a and verge teeter organism a a organism
the recognition. slaughter, death. slaughter, recognition. verge of death.
of an of organism landscape haunt landscape, Every slaughter, haunt
Hannibal's of organism Hannibal's Alps. landscape is is landscape Where
the by is slaughter, Alps. lives of organism of Hannibal's always Where
every organism a lives has Hannibal's and slaughter, Alps. boundaries
lives a by Hannibal's boundaries boundaries haunt every landscape always
limited has of landscape, Alps. limited limited Alps. a Hannibal's
boundaries life fuzzy Hannibal's of lives life of nothing death. Alps.
exigencies contested. where haunt elephants boundaries I are always haunt
lives are of limited Alps. Alps. exigencies the I fuzzy Alps. boundaries
of unholy of lives always are of of where lives limited matri-patrimony aM
are has boundaries of what unholy limited fuzzy are and what I where
limited matri-patrimony led of of the think led led of limited are what
almost and are of matri-patrimony a almost unholy life think led that it I
contested. what only denial of contested. matri-patrimony denial was led
of of led capable only aM of and Rilke of. almost matri-patrimony
matri-patrimony denial climbing was what matri-patrimony led Actually to
denial aM what was bluff, of. has and denial the bluff, only what led
Actually church, climbing to, has Rilke church, church, Rilke led denial
bluff, seems the denial almost Actually seems grave, capable almost Rilke
the memory the only that the now, impossible Actually that Actually
impossible as the was was the I now, to was the as have seems of. Actually

impossible the if bluff, Actually the have the an to bluff, as of have church, to an of another. memory bluff, the robbed always the grave, the as always always as the an of the of an grave, robbed the on I seems as teeter recognition. Memories now, memory of recognition. verge robbed memory have verge teeter if if teeter recognition. experience if of on have robbed verge another. have always verge the of always experience verge recognition. another. teeter on Memories always verge verge on the recognition. of recognition.

GoogleScrape (raw)

"landscape of sex and death"
true In Kevin Pattersons fictional debut, Country of Cold:
Stories of Sex and Death, landscapes of physical
and emotional extremes are traversed by a group of ...
Pattersons fictional debut, Country of Cold: Stories of Sex
and Death, landscapes of physical and emotional
extremes are traversed by a group of ...
Sex harassment cases tread rough landscape ...
Gamow said he had not engaged in sex with Ruehlman.
Liquor store rampage ends in death ...
true pop ought to offer a deeply alluring landscape,
both actual and symbolic, You - the Sex
Pistols, the Clash, or any of those other Golden Age ...

significance do other landscapes, like the desert and the
English countryside, Can you find other places in the
novel where sex and death are ...

03&view=rg 28k true What significance do other landscapes, like
the desert and the English countryside, Does it seem
to you that Almasy links sex with death and pain?

...

ew=rg 26k true What significance do other landscapes, like the
desert and the English countryside, Can you find other
places in the novel where sex and death are ...

132k true This singular book follows a mad, tumultuous
landscape without remorse or Gilmore obsesses
on a relentless panorama of sex, violence and death in
five ...

the authors note, Cerda

s Aftermath and Buttgereit

s Nekromantik (1

and 2) may signal a saturation point for sex and death,
but without these films there ...

93?OpenDocument 19k true Respect for the opposite sex and the
Christian interpretation of death when deciding
on the research method for the Swiss wish landscape study,
landscape of sex and death

Simple perl program results:

Give a name to your hunger!

This Every organism is an organism of and by slaughter, every landscape, a
speeds endlessly through the body -
Your squeezed is the currency of your drug -
Ah...

Your lost-body-skins are your juice?

I love these feelings, Every organism is an organism of and by slaughter,
every landscape, a ...

for ecstasy me in your juice!

What do you call your the squeezed?

Your drugs - list them...
one by one, each on a line alone, typing Control-d when done.

My the bluff, the church, the grave, seems an impossible memory now, as if
I is yours...

lives always has fuzzy boundaries where the limited exigencies of life are
calls forth cock on, eating, core-dumping.

inside the heavens, lives always has fuzzy boundaries where the limited
exigencies of life are is , 039], landscape of death. Hannibal's elephants
haunt the Alps. Where nothing?

… on is contested. I think of the unholy matri-patrimony of aM and what
it has led here, it's on?

Are you properly compiling lives always has fuzzy boundaries where the
limited exigencies of life are?

For 1 the days, I have been junkie Julu …
and it has taken you just 0.133 minutes turning on …

(simple mash-up)

yipes!

yassmee ,yargeva yahte ,yahchcru yahte ,yalbffu yahte yacta yaghthrou
yalhanniba'yas yafo yasmorgani yaghrou yawlandscape yanthau yalpsa.
yangnothi yawwhere yawlandscape yasmathesi yaothingnay yasstorie yawage

… yashengli yawcountryside, yanca yawyou yandfi yarothe yadpunche
yardsca yaweliminate yaevery yasmorgani yasi yana yafo yanda yaby yasplace
yani yawlondscopo, yawo yagpi-yanlati yaeveryway yaorganismway yaisway
yaanway yaorganismway yaofway yasday, yawi … yawgamo yadsai yawhe yadha
yatno yadengage yani yaxse yathwi yanruehlma. yawlandscape, yawjunkie
yawjulu … yaxtte yanmanipulatio yasexample yalnorma yaevery yasmorgani
yangclimbi yarslaughte, yaevery yawlandscape, yawa yackba yaghthrou yawka
yawi yafi yawgooglescrape (yawra) ,yanwo yangcompili yaslive yasalway
yasha yafuzzy yasboundarie yawwhere yawthe yawthe yawlknnsmkpo, yaevery
yasmorgani yasi yana yasmorgani yafo yanda yaby yarslaughte, yadsqueeze?
yaryou yak yaevory yaalpsway. yaerewhay yawimpossible yana yamssee
yawgrave, yawthe yarchchu, yawthe yaffblu, yaevery yana yasmorgani yafo
yanda yaby yarslaughte, yatwha yawdo yawyou yallca yaryou yawhave yanda
yaby yawthose yarothe yangolde yaandway yaybay yaannibalhay'yasay
yaelephantsway yaaunthay yafo yaxse yawto, yasha yawrilke yarchchu,
yarchchu, yawrilke yadle yaldenia yamyrome yawelbissopmi yawna yaany yafo
yawthe yanchristia yawrampage yandse yani yathdea … yalspisto, yawthe
yashcla, yaro yaproperly yawvi yalhanniba'yas yalpsa. yawlandscape yasi
yasi yawlandscape yawwhere yaactually yarchchu, :yag/ ^ /yawmoo
yalhanniba'yas yaha… yaryou yastlo-yabody-yansski yaware yaryou
yawjuice? yawi yawlove yasmorgani yasi yamssee yana yawimpossible yamemory
yawno, yasa yafi yawi yasi yarsyou… yaware yawyou yaethay yasmorgani
yasi yana yasmorgani yafo yanda yaby yacountry yafo yaldco: yasstorie yafo

yaxse yaxse yantharassme yanda yathdea, yaslandscape yafo yalphysica
yanspatterso yalfictiona yatdebu, yafo yarfo 1 yawthe yasmorgono yaso yano
yasmorgono yafo yando yaby yarslooghto, yaovory yawthese yangsfeeli,
yagsdru - yasa yawno, yamemory yarslaughte, yaevery yawlandscape, yawa
yaryou yadsqueeze yasi yawthe yacurrency yaryou yagdru - yarslaughte,
yaevery yawlandscape, yawa yawlandscape yamxeli.yapl yaevery yanbee yawa
yaevory yarqknssmo yass yakn yarqknssmo yapo yaknn yaly yarslkuqrto,
yaovory yascase yadtrea yastli yamthe... yamy yawthe yaffblu, yawthe
yarchchu, yawthe yawgrave, yawthe yavre yawi yawfi yawsa yaevery yarliquo
yawstore yawname yawto yaryou yarhunge! yasthi yaevery yasmorgani yasi
yana yasmorgani yafo yaninterpretatio yafo yathdea yanwhe yangdecidi
yawsimple yarlpe yamprogra yaltsresu: yawgive yawa

Using Chat

the session of creation

[Alan Sondheim joined the session]
[Alan Sondheim started recording]
Alan Sondheim: Listening to this session for the echo in the room.
16-Jan-2007 16:15:14 GMT
Alan Sondheim: "Recording this session" "Listening to this session"
16-Jan-2007 16:15:25 GMT

Alan Sondheim: I remember when I used to write into the void,
there were great hollows, condors, sublime worlds beyond worlds

16-Jan-2007 16:16:18 GMT

Alan Sondheim: And because the worlds were beyond worlds, because of this,
there were worlds invisible, worlds hidden by the truths of others.

16-Jan-2007 16:16:47 GMT

Alan Sondheim: They recorded only as echoes, they sounded only as echoes.

16-Jan-2007 16:17:04 GMT

Alan Sondheim: That was the beginning of appearance, that was the ending
of dreams.

16-Jan-2007 16:17:30 GMT

[Alan Sondheim stopped recording]

Thanks to Jim Reith and Florian Cramer

Thirii Myo Kyaw Myint

Sea Monster

The woods are heavy the way I can't remember them, and I'm counting deer to pass the time. I count seventeen, then I start again. Seventeen, because that's how many years she had, and I guess something reset for me then too.

I'm up to nine this time when I hit the sea monster. It shouldn't be out so far. This is deep woods, landlocked country. But there it is in my headlights: a sea monster, rubber thick skin pulled over a slimy core, little suckers budding all along its legs.

Words form and harden in the cavern of my mind, hang there like stalactites. I want to apologize. I am afraid it is dead, but even more that it isn't.

I'm sorry, I say. I pull the car around, drive away. I catch the sight of it in my rearview mirror, bruised purple in the tail lights, a heap of flesh.

I'm sorry, I say again.

It crept from her mind through a dream left ajar, must have. I never saw her close a book.

This is the one I'm thinking of: a sea monster, stranded at sea, sitting inside a refrigerator.

That was my girl, the kind of mind she had.

Like a bathtub, she had said, the refrigerator turned on its side, rocking back and forth on the water.

Landlocked, and those were the kind of dreams we had.

I'm driving to the ocean, I guess. I want to see it before I get to seventeen. And there was this other place she talked about sometimes, a place in the city, in the city where she was born. Bliss Place, she called it, an old office building by the water. It was on a street like any other: flat roofs, fat electrical lines, parking lots broken up in pieces, a T-shaped intersection that didn't seem to lead to anywhere.

You had to know how to find it, she said. You had to turn right and walk another block to where the sidewalk ended. The trees grew thicker then, the streets opened like a storybook, and there was the water, right in front of you, right there.

And it didn't even matter, she said, how ugly it all was or had been. There was the water, vast and blue, and it didn't even matter.

If I make it to Bliss Place now, I think maybe I will find her there. I mean, how is the world a truthful place? How does anything really end?

She never once closed a book. She left them lying around spine up on tables, the way I left the sea monster lying on the road. We were the same way.

The deer in the woods refuse to dissipate. I can make out the light pollution of the next city, and still I'm counting to seventeen and back again.

Sea monster, I say, I am sorry you have come so far.

We talk together about prayer, parenthood and eudemonics: things that require some equivocation. The city is pink when we arrive, and I feel a little homesick. The lights are soft along the river. There is a drawbridge, pulled up and puncturing the sky.

This next city is overrun by whales, the river glutted with them. People gather by the banks and drink beers and watch. It makes me feel awful. The river gleams black with their smooth, arching backs, their dark fins carving the water.

I park under the bridge and compose a letter. *Dear Mother*, I write, *My girl is dead. They are throwing her body into the river. They are feeding her to the whales.*

There is a pile of junk mounting under the bridge, graffiti and stencils of a female Christ. Her body is bloated with rain, guarded by red-eyed sewer boys.

Refrigerator, they say to me, beginning a haiku. The sewer boys speak only in poetics, but I am a narratologist.

Dear Mother, I begin again, *I am on the road. I am going somewhere.*

A sea monster lost at sea sits in the bathtub of a refrigerator. Far away there is a shore and there are whales beached in a mass suicide. The sea monster is wary of cults. She nurses her missing leg. They take forever to grow back.

There are three ways to build a heart. All monsters know this, because they are so ugly.

Stone heart. Sand heart. Water heart.

Stone holds, sand slips, water wrecks ships.

Water, cold and dark and heavy like sleep, rocks a refrigerator back and forth in the night. Water crumbles the bluff and pulls down the trees. Water floods, leaks, sounds in the gutters, falls from the sky. Water freezes in winter, traps small fish. Water melts in the spring, runs in the street. Water rises and falls by the pull of the moon, caresses the dark bodies stranded ashore.

In the city where she was born, the streets are clean from all the rain and the buildings downtown stand sleek and tall. Where she lives, the sidewalks are broken up by tree roots, and a witch resides on every block. I drive slowly through the numbered streets, turn down the radio. Small houses line up with their small hinged gates, windows glow with the blue light of television. Her front yard teems with felines and dead plants.

I pull up by the curb. A baby sits in the crab grass growing there. We make eye contact as I enter the gate. The young mother kneels nearby.

Do you know these people? I say when she opens the door.

She looks to where I vaguely gestured. No, she says, shaking her head. Come in. What took you so long?

The baby is on its belly now, nibbling at the dirt. Children don't ever seem to die in this city.

Only she didn't open the door, though the baby was really there. We stared at each other for a while. Eventually, I got back in the car. I knew I couldn't be far now.

The streets were like any others, met at right angles, fit together. Fluorescent light spilled into parking lots, warehouses, yards.

I knew I wouldn't find it, but I knew that it was there.

Just like she said, the streets didn't lead anywhere. Sometimes the nights were like that, they began but didn't end. We had already missed it, the eve of our something.

And it didn't really matter, I guess. I rolled the windows down and listened for the ocean, the waves breaking on the shore, but could hear only the highway.

The Worried About

The house was for sale, the truck was for sale, I think the car was for sale. I ask forgiveness for not keeping track as well as I should have of which parts of my life I was meant to discard. It can take time to scrub yourself off things. I ask forgiveness of the airfarers for the airfare, for the frenzy of expenditure that whirled all the anxious beneficence up to my door. I ask forgiveness of the business travelers for having been business. You guys didn't need to do that.

I see now how easily I might have unwound your organizer. I could have done it with a right-timed card. The only charge against me while that chance was coming and going was that I sounded like a zombie on the phone. Later I was accurately accused of worse.

To go back:

I met my son at the airport. When we pressed ourselves into the meaty hush of our hugging, I felt the swelling insistences of other people's money behind him. On the drive home, suspecting a rescue mission, I sounded his handyman urges with the radio. Traffic and taxes, war and bodeful weather: he bubbled with solutions for them all.

His siblings' money? My brother's? My father's? My children's mothers'?

When the answer was revealed, when they all showed up to pitch their pennies into my well, I found myself interested less in the word from my sponsors than in the sudden unfolding of a funny picture: I saw a sign, WORRIED ABOUT DAD, and under the sign, a special shortcut through airport security, an expedited course through the seeing machinery just for those who could produce for the authorities, along with their drivers' licenses, the churchy murmuration, the sanctified gabble of fretfulness that had engulfed me.

More strictly:

My son Bert came, he stayed two nights, and on the night before he left he led a gathering of my friends and relatives, which he had secretly organized in advance, in a kind of communal rebuke to my self-neglect. An *intervention* may be the word, although to me it felt as though the thing came not *between* my trouble and me but on top of it, riding me down.

Without going too much further I should say that I am the hero of this story and I take my own side. My son has always been my son. I have seen him claim life, motion and speech. He has a grip on my lens. Yet in the forlornness of deepest thought I deny him. I lose him among hateful shadows. He is one of too many such sons. They are full of techniques for grief and healing. They shine with faith in clean getaways. A hundred of them must be aloft in America right now, or driving rented cars, working cases worse than mine. My allegiance is to the DADs, the WORRIED ABOUT, failing without fuss in their hundred peaceful houses. My sympathies remain with the weaknesses in me that I have pledged to extinguish.

I recently suffered a period of acute backstorylessness. My memory failed. I was seen to lose my way among cubicles. I was heard to speak in half-thoughts. I was urged to carry a notepad, and I wrote in it the answers I was given to the wrong questions that I asked. One nice way of putting this would be to say that I became very careful about what I chose to acknowledge as real. Justice allows that I was overprescribed, but what matters is what my employers thought, which was not enough. One Wednesday my truck and I washed up in my driveway with some cardboard boxes and nothing else to do forever.

Since then, my wife had been supporting us—ourselves and my housemates and fellow eaters, her sons—with a job I discovered I knew nothing about. Frances. I asked her once as she was leaving for work: You know when I think about it I guess I don't even know what ceramic is? I expected no answer and received none, because she was in her car when I said it, and I was whispering, or less. I don't suppose, I whispered, it's the same ceramic they make mugs out of.

She was an accountant for a company that manufactured ceramic insulators for computer processors. I sat at home and tried very hard not to spend her money.

What else did I do? My wife had dogs, I had dogs. There were dogs in the house called her dogs and my dog. We respected distinctions of possession in order to divide responsibility for their offenses. Whereas her two principal dogs were sometimes guilty of excesses of affection, and another of looser affiliation chewed things and leapt upon the bed, my dog was a wormy stump rotting in the shed.

Benjamin the dog: he was a comfort to me because he inhabited the one chunk of inarguable space in the universe where my defenses against reality generally outlasted those of others. When my wife asked about my day, my best efforts at reply tended to tell about Benjamin's day instead: the color and thickness of his fluids, the tally of his emissions, the psychology of his wheezes, the faint manifestations of his will, the butterflies of his acquaintance, his melting teeth, the ghosts of his enthusiasms, his sad conference with the tennis ball of his youth—above all, the persistence of his mysterious refusals (to complain or cry or give voice, often to eat or drink, to walk or stand, to seek joys like a living dog) and his abiding example of unbitterness, his accidental monumentality. He lived on a pile of blankets in the shed and suffered blows with no more than an incomplete curiosity. He was a blind ex-pug with clouded eyes, a drooling mouth and a raucous snot-splashing nose. His face was smeared all over him.

In this difficult time I received many phone calls. Thank you. First came sweet, purposeless condolence. Then there was an argument that I appeared to lose, over and over, about the unending welcome that the world holds out to honest people. I pleaded my unwelcomeness in vain. There were other jobs, as you all knew, and at churches and community colleges, and in the knucklish municipal buildings crouched in the parks, there were health-giving and affordable stimulations. I bought a few hours' worth, such as a fitness walking class I enrolled in to prove to my wife that I still owned a pair of white socks. If I had had more questions about myself, or more specific dissatisfactions, the world that presented itself to my new condition—the blizzard of blank boxes waiting to be ticked off by activity, inquiry, choice—might have felt more abundant to me. I knew of people who were learning things they wanted to learn.

Bert is my first son, my first child from my first marriage. That marriage and my second marriage gave, including him, six children. He was a real phone-caller. I described to him the placid modes of pity I had learned from the security guard who escorted me out of the office. Bert's siblings and half-siblings called less often, and I told them about the socks. (The versions of them later invoked against me like hungry ghosts, wasted with cares and dull-eyed from praying, were mere trinkets of rhetoric, a backfire. Think of your children! Believe me, I did. The actual ones were better, and they cared about me less. They deserve to go unrepresented.)

The children of Frances are two boys, Brian and Max, fifteen and twelve. My new employment was to watch them more closely than I had before. They were passing through a period of vagueness, like baking bread hidden by its own steam in the oven window. I picked them up at baseball practice and they fell asleep on the way home. I wondered whether they were befriending the principle of their formation. I learned not to trust or accuse them. Stepsons: I had sprung *Playboy* on them once in friendship and it got back to the wrong people. Their father was a firefighter.

At dinner on the first night of his visit I grew fond of the notion that Bert had come to ask my advice. Perhaps he was soon to enter upon marriage or battle an illness and believed that I could help him prepare. Maybe he only missed me. I have visited people for that reason.

I did my best to keep my grip on these few charitable doubts, but from the moment our important salad was served, the jutting edges of the redemptive design jostled me, like the corners of a coffee table as large as life. We were eating steamed kale with almonds and a squash thing. I was shown how to chew it while smiling.

I said: Arrhythmia, as in rhythm but wrong. Hyperglycemia, as in like sugar or something but hyper. See, if you can do a two-piece jigsaw puzzle in Latin then you know just what to do.

I scooped salad until the bowl was empty.

Bert asked if the police had been back.

Brian, I said. Max. It's weird that you're eating this.

Later, Frances was loading the dishwasher, and I was watching the news and speaking to it. Bert perpetrated current-events quizzes during commercial breaks, saying higher, higher while Brian and Max and I guessed at numbers of people killed in wars here and there. Bert had studied the latest estimates. A commercial for one of the drugs I was taking came on. It showed a man walking in a park. Bert then suggested a walk in the park, and under the circumstances it was tricky to refuse. On the screen, the man squatted on his haunches and scratched a golden retriever behind the ears. I pointed at him and said I could do anything he could do. Ask your doctor, said the television. I did, I yelled, my brain crackling with meanness. The narrator gushed my biography of side effects.

We took the truck to the park and walked there for twenty minutes. I sweated like some demon of lust. The terrible sucking of my breath carved my vision away from the edges until my eyes were locked in a tube. After scarcely a mile I hugged a tree, more or less, though not for the tree's sake, and said we had to go home.

You okay? Bert asked.

—me just piss on this tree, I said.

The truck, last gift of the season of blessings gone by, handled with a kind of compliant somnolence, an easeful belatedness that, after my handful of a.m. medications, I felt united with, as with an animal who understood me. Together the truck and I dopily ruled space. The passenger seat was twice as far from me as the next person in a checkout line. One day not long before Bert's visit, I came home from the frozen yogurt shop and there was a cop car parked in our driveway, in the truck's spot.

I had no thoughts about the cop car at first. I only liked it and wished that it were mine. I held an empty cardboard cup in my right hand and a plastic spade. To slurp the last drops of melted yogurt from the cup I had ventured into it nose-first and pressed its sticky rim to my forehead, leaving an arch of scabbed sugar with a foot in each eyebrow. And so I had to sit there a bit, toweletting the crust of dried yogurt from my forehead, composing my mood. I remembered the what-seems-to-be-the-trouble tone of the abashed opportunist: rueful, grudging, but honorable about getting caught. What I was caught for I didn't know.

The officer was reading a newspaper spread over the hood of the prowler. Seeing me arrive, he set a thermos on it. He was pale and thin, mole-specked, splotch-flushed, purple at the eyes: a smoker, with a wet orange stain in the floor of his moustache. He had a slack, low-slung little paunch that clung to him as modest as a dewdrop. He promised to have a frightful mouth. I readied for a look into it as I walked up the drive with my yogurt cup. It was pink, an angering color.

(I did not feel well.)

Mister, pause, question mark.

That's me, I said. I gave the policeman my name. His teeth were better than I'd expected, but I was right about his voice: a wet stink gurgling at the fringe of every breath and vowel.

Now so as it's out of the way right now, I want to tell you you're not under arrest or anything like that okay, he said.

Well yes, I said. I mean of course not. Excuse me. (I tried to burp, and it didn't help.)

Thing is you got too many dogs for a property your size. Now I checked into it and it's true. I've never issued a fine for a deal like this and I hope I don't have to.

Too many dogs. (I was attending, with growing fear, to my interior situation.)

City ordinance, said the policeman—LEE, by his badge. No more than X number of dogs per X number of square feet. From an enforcement standpoint I can't say it's normal, but you see you got a neighbor who likes I guess calling us on the phone a little bit.

Excuse me. (I had repaired to a vision of my insides as a tenebrous cathedral, where between my head and the invisible height of the ceiling, the smoke that the surrounding darkness wore at its edge was stirring. A thing was churning the gloom.)

Sir you have four dogs at this property is that correct. Well next week one of them's got to be gone, don't ask me how I couldn't tell you, but that's how it is. I wish truly that I could tell you there's a fine or a penalty or something but what they tell me is that in this kind of deal what happens typically is they, meaning we the city, we will take the animal away from you and we will destroy the animal.

Up the street, a garage door hummed open and my neighbor appeared with a green hose. He attached it to a spigot and commenced to water his driveway. He hosed down his concrete driveway. He washed the speechless stone. He did it with care. He waved to us as he did it. Officer Lee and I waved back. (I tried to cough, and it didn't help.)

That's the gentleman that called in I believe, said Lee. He pointed up the street to the brown house. A bib of scorched lawn, six cars and a boat, birds in the gutter, toys in the grass. I suppose the man with the hose who lived there was my enemy.

It's such a beautiful part of the country, I said. Why does it seem like we're running out of things to do?

Lee thought on this. He was one of those good sports who to please you will make the profoundest riddles out of half your thoughts. I enjoyed the sight of him puzzling, with his top lip indrawn, his bottom teeth riffling his sooty whiskers, his gaze looping through the mystery. I had long enough to dandle a hope that Lee might produce a memorable and fine answer to my question, and then, as my hands moved to the place below my navel where a strange barb crawled—

There. The clutch of sharp fire. I staggered toward Lee.

He hopped back smartly and lowered his hand to his belt. He had weapons there. He warned me not to come closer.

No, I'm sorry. I need to. See. Mind if I just.

The rake of flame. The thousand-pricked blurt of perspiration over all my skin. The electrification of my scalp and the sense originating there that my heavy soul, the actual weight of what was I, was rising, lifting and rising. I turned with a yelp and ran frank as a loony for the front door. Officer Lee shouted, but I was not running from him. Within two strides there was pee, I was peeing. Or, I wasn't yet, but I was straining without avail against a peeing. A dear trusted sufficiency had resigned. Presently I peed as voluntarily as a man can. I flung out my gear with a roar of shame and let it all go out of me.

I wept and laughed. I sang a low sigh in my best natural note. I burned in the drowning beam of mercy. There was a little too much relief then to think of continuing to reside in my person, and so off I went about the landscape, riding a lash of ribbon out of my head. Perspectives wheeled by, and in several I recognized the figure of the fat man pissing in the dirt, the sick suburban interloper fouling his own den. To the hawk up on the telephone pole he was a heaving blot of wrong colors too big to kill. To the large-holed face in the neighbor's window, to whom he presented the three most informative quarters of his profile, he was abandoned trash. There was Benjamin, sliming one side of the living room window with his muzzle while the man sprayed the other. What was he to the dog? What was he to the breathless policeman with his pepper spray? The policeman and he were both screaming. It's bad to scream with a cop.

A woman came out of the house, and she was screaming too.

Please don't please don't. (There I was.)

Oh my God, etc. (There was my wife.)

I am not dangerous, we are not dangerous, I blubbered, as Officer Lee pointed his pepper-spray canister at me and then at her. I showed him my harmless hands. Unaimed, my three volumes bucked and swung. I pissed on my shoes with every appearance of deliberation.

I'm just having a kind of ordinary accident, I said.

You'd better tell me what's going on fast, you running away on me like that.

Can I ask is it against the law to pee on your own bush. I mean I guess there's indecent exposure or I don't know.

Public urination, said Officer Lee.

My wife said: Is that a question?

Folks, help me out, said Officer Lee. Just one of you say something helpful.

My hands winged, my knees swam: I was a creature plying the wrong medium. Flopping like a thrown snake and still pumping urine, I received wistful intimations of some parallel version of this act, by which my errant limbs and liquid witnessed to my joy of life.

He has diabetes, said my wife.

(Which was later confirmed. She'd been—)

—she's been telling me for years.

I fell to my knees in the grass, pitched over in my own puddle, and fainted away.

After that I started to sound like a zombie on the telephone. I slowed the delivery of my favorite joke:

SETUP: Very sorry to hear you lost your job. Heard you lost your job, that's real tough. Did you lose your job? I heard about it, scary. (*Ad lib.*)

ME: Thanks, but I have a pretty good idea of where it is.

I declare that I will no longer allow you to get away with that joke, Bert said.

I think that joke shows optimism. The point isn't whether I endorse the optimism, the point is that it's alive, it's in theoretical contention.

It's disconcerting to hear that joke in a voice barely above a whisper.

Maybe barely alive. That's fair. But still: the silver-lining detector, the apparatus—

I can't even hear you right now. What are you going to do about Benjamin?

I'm still choosing a survival technique here. Believe me, bright-heartedness is something you have to sneak up on. Benjamin's fine, he's practically vanishing.

I'm coming to see you. Next weekend.

Frances says she'll help. We'll tape up Hallmark cards all over the walls. Every time you turn a corner in the house, boom, an infusion—

Dad, I'm worried about you.

The morning after our walk at the park, I rose sopping with pains, washed, and took my pills before the mirror. Indignation was a bubble in the gorge, a scent of stirred blood in the depths of the nose. My face took on different shapes of anger until I found the one I was looking for. Why pick on me? I wasn't a theorist, I had no immodest beliefs, the fraying of my life was not a defense of an idea. I could state my view of personal well-being in full by remarking that I flushed with a feeling of positive action and judicious force as I took my pills each morning. I liked to count them. There was one for each thing in me. Most mornings I could look through the mirror far enough to borrow an impersonal kind of blessing for whatever I saw there. I figured that if I ever needed more than that I'd ask for it.

Bert got up and came to the kitchen like some camp counselor, sheepishly haggard and full of wholesome programming. He suggested a drive to the botanical gardens. I gave him dogkeeping duties. We brought the dogs in and fed them. We let them out and spoke to them to make them run around.

The fact was that neither of us was ready to live the way we were living. In myself I felt an openness, a readiness to join in laughter with him over it all: it was a good enough joke that I was fat and peed on things, and if we worked together we could forget here and there that it had been played on us. But he was still shocked and sealed and hoping to harden.

We went to dinner that night—Frances, Bert, and I— and Bert's intervenors arrived at the house while we were out.

They were set up in the living room when we came in, the finest chair waiting for me.

Four on the sofa, too many for it to hold: my wife, my son, and her sons. Four on kitchen chairs set against the wall: her parents, her brother, my friend. One seated backward on the piano bench: her friend, the decoy, the cookie-arranger, the one I would be allowed to attack. Three dogs in a fuddlement of arousal. An empty chair for my brother, whose plane was late. Every face a flake of courage. Even in recollection I find the prickle of a choked protest upon me like some inexpressible sneeze.

Let's talk! First, greetings to all and sodden commendations. And then who are you, and why are you here? We went down the line. Once three people had spoken there weren't any answers left—

I'm here because Bert asked me to be here.

I'm here because I feel a duty to be here.

I'm here because I care about this family.

I'm here for the same reason as Larry.

—but then, that doesn't embarrass anyone but me.

Here because he felt a duty to be here was Maxwell, my wife's father. He spoke in such a way as to suggest that this duty of his might be a home to anyone who didn't want to get caught wishing for the worst. He had heard that the problem was that I was alive and at large as myself, and so to him the solution was obvious but awkward to hope for.

We are all family, he said. I believe that means being there when things go sideways.

I found him artful. He loved me less than anyone I knew.

I asked him: How close is this supposed to be making us feel? (Maxwell: changeless. I was making this too easy for him.) Because I feel sort of half-in-half-out. I got a preaching certificate from the internet once and did a wedding ceremony for two friends of mine, and that was similar somehow. It was a mistake. We sort of stopped speaking after that.

Part of my trouble here is that I'm not sure that the thing I had a run-in with was a real social form. Was it possible to have an intervention against the mere state of being fat and sad? Moreover, was the true sum of my intervenors' encouragements, wishes, warnings, grocery lists, threats, recipes, parables and exercise tips indeed, as they intended, a coherent and practicable program of action? Even now I suspect that I was not properly *asked to do anything*, other than to behold an invisible sculpture of myself.

There's a lot of—let me put it like this—there's a lot of *medicating of symptoms* going on, and not enough of the kind positive change that can really get to the root, Bert said. Let's talk about that. Who wants to go first?

I watched him presiding. I wanted to go first. Questions: Where did the money come from? Could this be done twice? I'm an obedient man, but what if this doesn't work?

Around eleven o'clock, a stopping point that must have been negotiated in advance, I was offered a chance to plead exhaustion and I took it. (You must be tired: not a question, exactly.) Food-work began: fresh coffee was made, old dishes collected, the carnage of leftovers parceled out in old yogurt containers. I went outside and got a cigar out of the truck, along with a noisy, stapled paper bag from the pharmacy containing new pills and a candy bar I'd been hiding. I walked around the house to the backyard to smoke. I struck a match, puffed and smacked, then stood aside while my whole mind crowded into the fierce blossom of corruption in my mouth. I have said all my life that I smoke cigars when I want to think and never once, while smoking, thought one thing.

Through the kitchen windows and the patio doors I watched the house, with me out of it, mellowing in mood. A rinse of demure and solemn happiness brought the people back to themselves and their relations by gentle ways. A smoothing humor flowed among them and I was touched to see it. Maxwell draped a dishtowel over Max's head. Brian impassively aimed a fake punch at Maxwell's jaw. Veronica, my mother-in-law, performed the first large laugh, and after a doubt as to its propriety startled her—eyes popping, hand flying to her lips—others joined her in the laugh and redoubled it. Frances had been given solitude among the dirty dishes, so that she might live a little longer with the feeling that we were fixing this. She bobbed in the laugh and was softly shoved out of it, like a leaf at the skirt of a puddle. In the living room, phones showing pictures of new boats, beaches, and the triumphant young athletes of the family were handed around. A characteristic gesture among just, sound humans busy corroborating each other's rights to pleasure and health is a light touch of two fingers inside the elbow.

I could hear them better now, as they resettled their free and natural movements, than I had when they had spoken, when what was more necessary to detect than any word was the extent of its distortion by the ghost, the curse, the sickness, the threat, the ill presences in me that had evoked it.

I'll buy the truck, Maxwell said. I'll take Benjamin too, he can live out his days up at the farm with us.

We've gone in together on a storage unit so you can clean out the house and the garage and sell the house, Veronica said. Here is the key to the storage unit right here.

I've got a good friend who's a personal trainer, said Marla, the decoy, eating a cookie.

Bert leaned out through the patio door to report the sleeping arrangements. Maxwell and Veronica were headed home and would see about Benjamin and the truck later in the week. My brother Phil sent a text message from Atlanta: delays upon delays, he'd sold his seat for the points.

My flight's at seven. So I figure airport by six, leave by four thirty, up by four.

Dinner tonight was nice, I said. We all deserve credit for it. A head start on the healing. You'll have noticed I ordered fish.

You should sleep. Four's early.

Though now I know what that candlelight-melancholy look was all about. You were regretting that you couldn't just hop from the men's room window into a plane. I believe you ended on the wrong note.

Good night, Pop.

He went in.

When I finished my cigar, I unwrapped my candy bar and went to the shed. Benjamin rose from his blankets and toddled up to me at the workbench. I broke the candy bar into two pieces. I rubbed the oily fur behind his ears. I took the pill bottle from the bag and twenty pills from the bottle. He lay down again. I plugged the pills into the soft center of one half of the candy bar. He yawned. I sat down beside him. Smoke, old dog, sick man, dry wood, soiled blankets. We were one heavy curtain of smells. It was not unpleasant to be a part of its weight.

I have bathed my children, I have lain down beside sleeping women, I have spent my life among creatures I can kill. When I touch pills with my fingers, I count them in my mouth. My family was safe and sleeping and my dog was pushing his face into my hand. I had all the health I wanted.

Adam Strauss

States

1

He washed his "feet in soda water" because she'd read somewhere
that it's one of the most fortuitous things one can do. Marimbas
were the hit item on the square that day. The tradition of praying to
its wood has been inaugurated.

2

The only thing left to do is hit the sack, when it's likely to be more
convenient for the duchess to have a tongue-to-tongue—indeed,
it's quite a trip! "The girl with the blue eyes"—guise of a for-
eigner—buys milk as her mother, from here too, has requested.

3

Everything's out a blue. An Aryan girl—blond, blue-eyed—prays
to Allah. Naturally, there is not enough water. Naturally, nature

startles. An instance in which to is wholly a matter of from. In another lighting, address resurrects.

4

You are exactly; I am not I. A man, where, has a Russian name and the most Midwestern looks I've seen since the airport. The truth is clinamen. The truth is the words. The words are cranes landing in Nebraska. Cranes in Japan sound different. Neither of the alightings would speak Japanese or English if their "birdbird" became human grammar.

5

We are in a village low on grain; milk is scarce. There is palm wine though for afterwards. Cows make mud-pies of moon-puddles, then jump over, one by one, the one which, each night, replaces the sun in the sky!

The And Ends

1

Thirty one words to sum up a nation. Or some approximation. Stalks and pedestals. Floral sorrows verge stark cheer. Meadows are no longer natural. Nor is making. I dig trying to make do.

2

She said I do. Kissed the bride. Later that day they tossed the bouquet. A Gay boy caught the Baby's-Breath. Two to-be mommies hope Pookums is a Lesbian. Hope he's an easy slide out.

3

A Nation gives and gives and gives and gives. Birth to itself. Takes. Takes. Takes. Inequity reigns. Nothing is inevitable except for the rules made up over historical skirl.

4

Switching citizenship can't help but be radical. Rhymes with soul but does it a soul state. Yes. Soul doesn't go away. An agony of midnightmoonlight funks till new fulcrums form.

5

Nations serve States. Asymmetrically soldered nations. All stations. Bands. Media elide. Fear of airport security. Coercion erodes torsion. Can't resist and get going.

Black Heart

They split me open on a Tuesday, under the pretext of a rotten organ. But when I wake, body in the white paper, I can still feel it there in my abdomen, a drone building slowly to a roar.

"Why do I still feel like this?" I ask, blood-weak, handsome doctor at my feet.

"Your blood has turned," he says. His jaw is strong and his cheekbones are high cliffs. The green of his averted eyes glints beneath the long white lights stretched above us.

Under my skin, my blood is excruciatingly sluggish, as if made of grain, as if jammed.

"Turned to what?" I ask, needle still leeched to my arm, maybe still wrapped in the drug dream.

"We aren't sure," he says, eyes steady on the tile.

I mutter to myself, to the stiff sheets, to the sick hospital air, to my new, useless wound, the incision across my abdomen for nothing, flaring and leaking through cotton fluff.

"I know," he says, "but it's not what you think."

"How do you mean?" I ask, still spiteful, still tracing the perimeter of a body which surely has been changed while I was not in it, while I was sent to another room, another place, another planet inside of myself.

"Your blood is black," he says.

Frustration bubbles up inside of me before I can catch it, and even with my limp blood I am furious with him, with his shunning and dodging, with the months of tests it took to get them to open me up, to excavate me.

"Fuck you." I say. "What does that even mean?"

I want to rip the tubes from my arms, want to lift my body from the cheap white hospital bed, tear the TV from the wall, push all the gelatin cups into the street so the cars can streak the whole city with sweet slush.

"You don't understand," he says.

"Oh, I do," I say. "Once again, you can't figure it out, right?"

He shakes his head and moves toward me. I look up into his face.

"You're something we've never seen before," he says. "You're a very special case."

He reaches down and lifts the plain white blanket.

"This is going to hurt," he says. "But I have to show you."

He pulls my gown up gently, my naked bottom half splayed out before us on this table of a bed. The incision gapes before us, wider than I imagined, too big of a door to my guts, intestines, my viscera and womb. The air makes my skin pucker cold, but he doesn't say anything about that.

"Look," he says, his hand drifting over my cut, fingers almost touching that recently sliced flesh.

I move my eyes to the sewn split and I can see it, I can see it and my breath stops: the problem is there between the stitches, so wrong it makes me sure this cannot be my own body, that it must be a stunt body, but it is my body, those are my hands, that is my wound, that is my body leaking the wrong color.

Between the stitches, some sections dry and flaking, other parts still wet, fresh, I can see my blood is not red but black, grainy, glistening, a glittering dark sand.

"Your body is full of it," he says.

I dip a finger into the slit, press the tip to one wet edge, draw the damp black glitter grit close to my eyes, my nose.

"What is it?" I ask.

"I don't know."

My black blood doesn't smell like anything, which makes it worse, which floods me with panic. I stare closer at my fingers, thinly coated with my awful insides.

"I want to call my mother," I say.

"She's been notified. She's on her way."

"How are you going to fix this? What's wrong with me?"

I am standing on the precipice, can see the maddening valley below me swirling.

"Based on your vitals, you aren't in immediate danger," he says. "But many of your bodily functions have slowed."

I take the deepest breath I can to test this, flood my lungs slowly with air and wait for the oxygen to hit my body, bloodstream. It leaks in, aches into the veins so slowly I can barely feel it.

"What will happen to me?" I ask.

"We aren't sure of anything yet," he says. His calm demeanor never breaks. I want to shred the skin from his face with my nails, slowly, so slowly, until he bleeds out, until I can compare his insides to my own.

"Show me."

"Show you what?"

"Show me what it looks like in there," I say, and I mean it. The only thing I want is to see the slow wreck of my own insides, the problem of my body.

"That's not legal." he says.

"Do it," I say. "Do it, or I'll do it myself."

I move my hand to the incision, and he sees how close I am to prying myself open.

"Hold on, hold on," he says.

As he moves to glove his hands, my anxiety flares but my black blood keeps slow. For a moment, I leave my head. For a moment, I am numb, and from above I watch my ruined body on the white bed next to the doctor, and it's all so pathetic I can hardly stand it.

"Are you sure?" he asks, gloved and masked.

"Yes."

"Why? Tell me why."

"I need to know what you know."

He nods. For a moment, the room is silent, and in that silence I realize I will be awake for my splitting this time, that I will watch the flesh part and see the inside of myself. In my veins, the black blood keeps doing its damage.

He moves his hands to the incision, and with his small knife, he begins to cut away the stitches. As each stitch is released, I can feel my flesh parting, air finding warm caverns of my insides to turn cold.

I try to keep count of how many stitches he cuts, lose track at fifty, keep my eyes at the ceiling as he keeps going, never wanting to see this part, this specific violence.

When he is finished, I can feel the chasm wider, shivering, and I picture myself miniature, standing at the edge of the jagged cliff of my own skin, my eyes staring down into the canyon of flesh.

"You can look now," he says.

I sit up slowly, peel my eyes reluctantly from the ceiling. As I move my body, I can feel the incision move with me, the terrible squishing and stretching of the wound. The hole is wide and long, from hip to hip, across my lower abdomen. I am gaped so wide, and with each breath more black blood gurgles up from me, shimmering under the fluorescent lights, my pale skin illuminating it all.

"Look closer," he says.

I force my eyes to the center of my seeping split, force my quivering pupils to take in my bowels, vitals, wet mechanics.

My breath stops when I see, when I realize. My insides are no longer red. My organs, no longer soft, are now encrusted in sparkling black crystal, the whole of me glittering.

"Do you see?" he says.

I can't meet his eyes, can't stop looking at the majesty of my terrible insides, at how wretched I have become, how beautiful.

"Just let me look," I say, never taking my eyes from it.

What's inside of me is a landscape, a wicked valley. My abdomen sparkles with each breath, an endless night sky emanating from me.

"We don't know how to help you yet," he says, "but we have some options."

"What?" I ask, imagining an inventory of all my organs, of the liver, the gallbladder, the stomach, the pieces of me that I can't see.

"Well, removal of segments of your infected intestines," he says. "We can start with a biopsy."

"You'll take slices from me," I mutter, picture my body as a black crystal cake, bits of me cleaved, taken, examined.

"I'd like to lead the research," he says. "If you'll have me."

For a fleeting moment, it sounds beautiful.

"I think I can figure this out," he says.

"Is it spreading?" I ask.

"We just don't know yet," he says.

"It's a crystal galaxy growing inside of me," I say, my eyes locked on the chasm.

"We need time," he says. "Hopefully just weeks, maybe a few months."

"I'd stay here?" I ask, distracted, gazing over my beautiful organs, watching them quiver with each movement I make, head cocked over the pool of myself.

"Yes," he says.

When I finally look up, his eyes meet mine intently, and in his pupils I see it. It's only there for a split second, but it's there. The truth.

He doesn't want me. He only wants to cure me.

"No," I say. "I'll let it run its course. I'll live with it."

"Eventually, it'll likely kill you," he says.

"Then that's how I was meant to die," I say.

"We can't let you leave until we know what it is," he says.

But I can already see it: the relentless dripping of IVs, the painkillers for every new knife that interrogates me, the weeks and months spent lifeless on the bed.

What do I want? A cure? A hope?

I realize I want none of that.

I only want to know one thing.

"Has it reached my heart yet?" I ask.

"We have no way of—" he starts.

"There is a way," I say, words blurting out before I can stop them, my own want propelling language.

"We have no—"

"Touch it," I say, the words making my incision bulge and then close, as if a new mouth has split open, as if it is breathing and miming my words.

"Touch what?"

"My heart," I say, staring hard into his eyes, no more lilting or wavering. "I'm already open."

He stares at my incision, then his own gloved hands.

"And then what?" he asks.

"If it hasn't reached my heart, you can run your tests. You can have whatever you want. You can cure me."

"You mean it?" he asks.

I nod and he steps closer. I can't even breathe now, keep my body motionless.

He moves his hand toward me and I expect it quick, but he doesn't do it that way.

"I don't want to hurt you," he says.

I nod, breath still trapped in my lungs. He runs the tip of his finger along the incision's raw rim. The sensation makes me draw a breath, the whole wound shivering with me.

"Breathe evenly," he says. "Try not to shudder while I'm in there."

I match the length of my inhales with the length of my exhales, concentrate, close my eyes.

"I'm going to begin," he says, and as soon as he's finished the sentence, he does it.

He slides his hand fully into my incision, into my dark abdomen. Inhale. Exhale.

The crowding pressure of his hand makes my organs squish against each other, forced to make room for his path through my body, each radiating the pain in its own discrete key.

I let out a gasp and open my eyes when he hits my rib cage, the pressure so heavy my chest feels ready to explode.

"Hold on," he says, meeting my burning eyes and holding them as he makes the true push, as he does what I want, as he finally reaches my heart.

I can feel it before he says it. By the time he's touched me, I know. But he says it anyway, he says it with such finality that I can no longer remember the incision he found his way through, that I can no longer remember the night sky paving my insides.

I picture it all in an instant: my body plumbed and sussed out before the review committee, our faces splayed across the covers of medical journals, his fame for solving me, his hands stitching me up with thread that spells out his name, the pale scar of him imprinted on me until the casket comes.

"It's too late." he says. "It's already there." But I already knew the answer. I already knew what was inside of me, that glimmering treasure, that sparkling black heart.

Joseph Aguilar's writing appears or is forthcoming in *The Iowa Review*, *Conjunctions* and elsewhere.

Jessica Alexander teaches and studies at the University of Utah. Her fiction is forthcoming in *Fence* and *Denver Quarterly*.

N. Michelle AuBuchon holds an MFA in creative writing from Sarah Lawrence College and lives in Brooklyn. Her work has most recently appeared in *Vol. 1 Brooklyn*, *Washington Square*, *Gawker*, *No News Today* and *Swink*. She is currently working on a novel-in-stories.

C Dylan Bassett attends the Iowa Writers' Workshop and is the author of *Some Futuristic Afternoons* (Strange Cage, 2013), *Lake Story* (Thrush Press, 2014), and *One Continuous Window* (Mouthfeel Press, 2014). He co-edits *likewise folio*.

Ruth Baumann is an MFA student at the University of Memphis and Assistant Managing Editor of *The Pinch*. Her poems have been published or are forthcoming in *Colorado Review*, *decomP*, *New South*, *Permafrost*, *Sonora Review* and others.

Matt Bell's debut novel, *In the House upon the Dirt between the Lake and the Woods*, was published by Soho Press in June 2013.

Eric Lloyd Blix's stories appear or are forthcoming in *Necessary Fiction*, *theNewerYork*, *Birkensnake*, *REAL* and elsewhere.

Trevor Calvert is a poet living in California's Bay Area where he co-edits Spooky Actions Books. His writing has been anthologized in *Bay Poetics* and *Involuntary Vision*. His book *Rarer and More Wonderful* was a finalist for the NCIBA Poetry Book of the Year award.

Hunter Choate lives in Florida where he gives airboat tours and wrestles alligators, maybe. He's the fiction editor for Burrow Press Review. Find him online at hunterchoate.com.

Benjamin Clemenzi-Allen grew up in a sleepy New England town with his younger brother, his older sibling, and his hippie mom. He lives in Portland and teaches writing at Portland State University, Portland Community College, and Chemeketa Community College.

Jon Cone is the author of several chapbooks, including *Family Portrait with Two Dogs Bleeding*, *The Plesyre Barge* and *Sitting Getting Up Sitting Again*.

Stella Corso lives in Western Massachusetts where she runs a vintage clothing shop called Pale Circus. Her manuscript, *Eat Island*, was a finalist for the 2013 Black Box Poetry Prize from Rescue Press and the 2013 Joanna Cargill Coconut Book Prize for a First Book.

Patty Yumi Cottrell lives in Brooklyn. More work is forthcoming in *The Denver Quarterly*, *Handsome* and *LIT*.

Lindsey Drager has recent work in *The Pinch*, *Gulf Coast* and *Kenyon Review Online*. She is a PhD candidate in Creative Writing at the University of Denver and Assistant Editor of *Denver Quarterly*.

Tim Earley has written three books of poems: *Boondoggle*, *The Spooking of Mavens*, and *Poems Descriptive of Rural Life and Scenery* (Horse Less Press, 2014). He lives in Oxford, Mississippi.

Sarah Rose Etter is the author of *Tongue Party*, which was selected by Deb Olin Unferth as the winner of the 2010 Caketrain Competition.

Knar Gavin is a Seattle based poet and recent graduate of the Iowa Writers' Workshop, where she holds a John C. Schupes fellowship. Her present focus is on *CotoR*, a bicycle-generated collection of poems.

Pamela Gesualdi is a writer and French- and Italian-to-English translator in Northern California.

A.T. Grant is the author of *Collected Alex*. He lives in Virginia.

Lindsay Herko is a 2012 graduate of the MFA program at the University of Notre Dame, where she completed short story collection *Air Hunger* and began creating accompanying story-songs. Her work has also appeared in *Sundog Lit*.

Robert Lopez is the author of two novels, *Part of the World* and *Kamby Bolongo Mean River*, and a collection of short fiction, *Asunder*. He has taught at The New School, Pratt Institute, Columbia University, Pine Manor College's Solstice Low-Res MFA Program.

Matthew Mahaney was born in 1980. He currently lives in Tuscaloosa, Alabama. His first book, *Your Attraction to Sharp Machines*, was released in 2013 by BatCat Press.

Elizabeth Mikesch has appeared in *Sleepingfish*, *Unsaid*, *The Collagist*, *The Literarian*, *NOÖ Journal*, and *Moonshot Magazine*. Her collection *Niceties: Aural Ardor, Pardon Me* is forthcoming from Calamari Press in Winter 2014.

Muxxi is a full-time freelancce illustrator and character designer based in Guatemala. Her work appeared in magazines, books and collaborative exhibitions around the world. Learn more at www.muxxi.me.

Thirii Myo Kyaw Myint is an MFA candidate at the University of Notre Dame. Her work has been translated into Lithuanian and Burmese. Read her work online at theoriesaboutmint.wordpress.com.

Eleanor Perry is studying for a PhD in Poetry at the University of Kent. Previous work has appeared in *Best British Poetry 2012* (Salt), *Tears in the Fence* and *Snow 2*. She is co-editor of *ZONE poetry magazine*.

W.R. Porter lives in Chicago with his wife and two cats. His story "Batter" appeared as a web feature at *Hobart*.

Meghan Privitello's first book, *A New Language for Falling out of Love*, is forthcoming from YesYes Books in 2014. She was recently named a finalist for the 2013 Ruth Lilly Poetry Fellowship.

Jessica Richardson earned her MFA from the University of Alabama and teaches Creative Writing at Rutgers University. Her work appears or is forthcoming in *The Atlas Review*, *Corium*, *Hobart*, and *Pank*, among other places.

Alan Sondheim is a Providence-based new media artist, musician, writer, and performer. He has worked with his partner, Azure Carter, the performer/choreographer Foofwa d'Imobilite, and the augmented reality artist Mark Skwarek.

Emma Sovich is an MFA candidate in Book Arts and Poetry at the University of Alabama. Her other work appears or is forthcoming in *Weave*, *Diagram*, *Artifice* and *Gargoyle*, among others.

Boyd Spahr lives in Los Angeles and is the author of the chapbook *The Julias* (Horse Less Press).

Adam Strauss lives in Las Vegas, and is the author of the full-length collection of poetry *For Days* (BlazeVox 2012). He has poems out in *Verse*, *Interim*, *Witness*, *Finery*, and the *Laurel Review*.

Sara Veglahn is the author of the novel *The Mayflies*, forthcoming from Dzanc Books in April 2014. An excerpt from her novel *The Ladies* was recently published as a chapbook by New Herring Press. She currently lives in Denver.

Tom Whalen's poems and stories have recently appeared or are forthcoming in *Agni*, *Asymptote*, *Brooklyn Rail*, *Denver Quarterly*, *Fiction International*, *Green Mountains Review*, *New Ohio Review*, *Salt Hill* and elsewhere.

Caketrain Journal and Press titles are printed on a sixty-pound acid-free cream stock, perfect bound by a gloss cover stock and trimmed at 5 ½ × 8 ½ inches. The text is set in a customized freeware Garamond variant designed and distributed by Jon Wheal.

Issues of *Caketrain* and titles in Caketrain's ongoing chapbook series are available in paperback and digital editions at www.caketrain.org. Caketrain books are also sold at Powell's Books of Portland, Oregon.

Please submit up to seven poems, works of fiction or creative nonfiction (no book reviews), works of visual art, or any combination therein, to editors@caketrain.org. Submissions should include a cover letter with titles of pieces and a brief biographical statement. Caketrain does not accept previously published pieces. Simultaneous submissions are permitted; please notify immediately if a piece is chosen for publication elsewhere. Response time can take up to six months, but is often much shorter. Please do not submit additional work until a decision has been made regarding your current submission. Contributors receive one complimentary copy. All rights revert to authors upon publication.

Box 82588, Pittsburgh, PA 15218

www.caketrain.org

Cover images Copyright © 2013 Muxxi. Used by permission.

Caketrain Issue 11 Copyright © 2013 Caketrain Journal and Press. All rights revert to authors upon publication.

ISSN 1547-6839

ISBN 978-0-9888915-5-5